"*Haunting Jasmine* is the kind of book that makes me remember all the reasons I love to read. Anjali Banerjee writes in luminous prose about the deepest secrets of a woman's heart. With a freshness of voice and a playfulness of the imagination, she brings her quirky characters to life. The gorgeous and multilayered language illuminates a story that will haunt the reader long after the final page is turned."

—Susan Wiggs, *New York Times* bestselling author

Jasmine, come home . . .

I take a deep breath and drag my suitcase up the narrow steps to the back door, which is now the main entrance to the bookstore. A well-worn path leads around the house to the ornate front door facing the waterfront, recalling a bygone era when important guests arrived by sea.

As I push open the back door, soft voices float toward me. The words coalesce, then change their minds and drift away. Inside the foyer, I'm submerged in dimness, save the faint orange glow from a Tiffany lamp. The heavy door slams behind me, shutting out the world . . . The air hangs heavy with expectation.

Jasmine, you're finally here, the house seems to say . . .

Further praise for Anjali Banerjee and her novels:

"Fresh and highly entertaining. I loved every word."

—Susan Elizabeth Phillips, *New York Times* bestselling author

"A masala-scented *Like Water for Chocolate*."

continued . . .

"Delectable . . . recounted with hilarity and warmth."

—*The Seattle Post-Intelligencer*

"This book has a romantic, magical quality."   —*Booklist*

"Fascinating, insightful, and delightful. The descriptions shimmer and sparkle. I intend to rush out and buy a copy for every woman I know."

—Jayne Ann Krentz, *New York Times* bestselling author

"The author's hip-hot style combines breezy storytelling, wry humor, and just enough poignant sauce in a romantic comedy equal to *Bend It Like Beckham*."   —*The Seattle Times*

"A *Bridget Jones's Diary* meets *Monsoon Wedding*–style escapade."

—*Publishers Weekly*

Haunting Jasmine

ANJALI BANERJEE

BERKLEY BOOKS, NEW YORK

THE BERKLEY PUBLISHING GROUP
Published by the Penguin Group
Penguin Group (USA) Inc.
375 Hudson Street, New York, New York 10014, USA
Penguin Group (Canada), 90 Eglinton Avenue East, Suite 700, Toronto, Ontario M4P 2Y3, Canada
(a division of Pearson Penguin Canada Inc.)
Penguin Books Ltd., 80 Strand, London WC2R 0RL, England
Penguin Group Ireland, 25 St. Stephen's Green, Dublin 2, Ireland (a division of Penguin Books Ltd.)
Penguin Group (Australia), 250 Camberwell Road, Camberwell, Victoria 3124, Australia
(a division of Pearson Australia Group Pty. Ltd.)
Penguin Books India Pvt. Ltd., 11 Community Centre, Panchsheel Park, New Delhi—110 017, India
Penguin Group (NZ), 67 Apollo Drive, Rosedale, North Shore 0632, New Zealand
(a division of Pearson New Zealand Ltd.)
Penguin Books (South Africa) (Pty.) Ltd., 24 Sturdee Avenue, Rosebank, Johannesburg 2196,
South Africa

Penguin Books Ltd., Registered Offices: 80 Strand, London WC2R 0RL, England

This book is an original publication of The Berkley Publishing Group.

This is a work of fiction. Names, characters, places, and incidents either are the product of the author's imagination or are used fictitiously, and any resemblance to actual persons, living or dead, business establishments, events, or locales is entirely coincidental. The publisher does not have any control over and does not assume responsibility for author or third-party websites or their content.

PRINTING HISTORY
Berkley trade paperback edition / February 2011

Library of Congress Cataloging-in-Publication Data

Banerjee, Anjali.
    Haunting Jasmine / Anjali Banerjee.
        p.   cm.
    ISBN 978-0-425-23871-4
    1. Young women—Fiction.   2. Booksellers and bookselling—Fiction.   3. Islands—
Fiction.   4. Puget Sound Region (Wash.)—Fiction.   I. Title.
    PS3602.A6355H38 2011
    813'.6—dc22

                                                                                    2010023024

PRINTED IN THE UNITED STATES OF AMERICA

10   9   8   7   6   5   4   3   2   1

In memory of my friend Keith Curtiss

acknowledgments

I am deeply grateful to the following people: my agent, Kevan Lyon, for her support and wisdom, and her colleague Jill Marsal. My editor, Wendy McCurdy, for her brilliance. Her highly competent assistant, Katherine Pelz, and the talented people at Berkley who have worked diligently on behalf of this book: art director Annette Fiore, copywriter Jim Poling, managing editor Jessica McDonnell, and copyeditor Sheila Moody. The esteemed Leslie Gelbman, president and publisher of Berkley Books. My fabulous critique group—Susan Wiggs, Elsa Watson, Kate Breslin, Suzanne Selfors, Sheila Rabe, Carol Cassella. The amazing Michael Hauge, for helping me find the story. Nathan Burgoine, for generously sharing his experiences as a bookseller. Rebecca Guthrie and everyone at Bethel Avenue Book Company. Lyn Playle, for the tour of the Walker-Ames Mansion, on which Auntie's Bookstore was loosely based. Stephanie Lile, for great talks while walking. The Brainstormers, including but not limited to: Gwynn Rogers, Pat Stricklin, Carol Caldwell, Carol Wissmann, Terrel Hoffman, Jan Symonds, Sandi Hill, Dee Marie, Theo Gustafson, Penny Percenti, Elizabeth Corcoran Murray, Soudabeh Pourarien, and all

ACKNOWLEDGMENTS

the Friday Teasters. Anita LaRae, for her insight. Susan Neal, for great ideas. Karen Brown, Kristin von Kreisler, Michael Donnelly, Sherill Leonardi, Casandra Firman, and Skip Morris, for perceptive reads of early chapters. Carol Ann Morris, for performing photo magic. Lois Faye Dyer, Rose Marie Harris, Julie Hughes, Renee Breaux. Claire Tomalin's book *Jane Austen: A Life* for details about Jane Austen. Last but never least, my family: my parents, Randy, Daniela, my siblings, nieces and nephews; Mom and family in Texas. My cat companions, and my husband, Joseph, as always.

Chapter 1

I didn't see this turn of events coming, or going. My ex-husband, Rob, used his charm like a weapon, and ultimately he didn't care whose heart he broke—or whose life he ruined. Neither did he care whose bed he woke up in. My mother would say, *Well, Jasmine, that's an American penis for you. You should've married a Bengali. Faithful, good, and true to his culture.* Her words conjure an image of the royal Bengali penis decked out in a traditional *churidar kurta*, its head peeking from the gold-embroidered white silk *kurta* at our traditional Indian wedding. But my mother won't get her wish—I won't marry again.

Now that the divorce is final, I need a break from L.A., from the errant ex-husband whom I once thought was perfect. I'm alone on the ferry to Shelter Island, a green dot of rain-soaked darkness in the middle of Puget Sound. Out on the boat's breezeway, the wind whips my hair, reminding me that I'm still alive, that I can still feel the cold. Robert's number pops up on my cell phone screen—the green digits that I have come to loathe. I ignore the call and send him into the barren wasteland of Voice Mail. Let him deal with the real estate agent and the vultures descending on the condo. I've made my temporary escape into solitude.

As we approach the island, the eastern shoreline emerges from a wall of fog. Madrone and fir trees tumble down to wild rocky beaches; forested hillsides rise into pewter skies; and the town of Fairport hugs the harbor in a density of antique buildings and twinkling lights. My heartbeat thuds. What am I doing here? Soon the moss will grow between my fingers, in the creases of my nose, and in the pockets of my thin raincoat, where I keep Auntie's letter, her urgent request that summoned me home.

In the age of e-mail, she prefers to write the old-fashioned way. I pull her note from its hiding place and sniff the paper— a faint scent of rose. Each time I unfold the letter, the fragrance changes. Yesterday it was sandalwood; the day before, jasmine. But the words remain the same, written in Auntie's slanted golden script:

> I must go to India. I need you to run the bookstore while I'm away. Only you will do.

When I called her to ask, *Why me?* she mentioned "fixing her health" in Kolkata. She wouldn't say more, but how could

I deny my fragile old auntie? She promised me refuge among the classics, although I haven't had time to read a novel in years. The evidence hides in my oversized handbag—a rolled-up copy of *Forbes* magazine and a cell phone, a Black-Berry, and a netbook. The weight of technology pulls on the shoulder strap. I barely have room for the usual supplies—compact, lipstick, tissue, aspirin, allergy pills, charge cards, receipts, and a bundle of keys, including one that opens the exercise room at the office. Not a single novel, and yet, what do I have to lose? How hard can it be to sell the latest Nora Roberts or Mary Higgins Clark?

A month on the island, sitting in the bookstore, is a small enough sacrifice for my beloved auntie. I brought work to keep me occupied, including a roll of green bar reports that I haven't had time to review.

As the ferry docks, a gust of wind snatches Auntie's letter from my hand. The pink paper flutters into the water, and for a moment her handwriting glows in the evening light, then dissolves into sparkles as the letter sinks. I consider diving in after it—drowning would be a welcome release from sorrow. But a seagull calls out, admonishing me to keep my chin up, to defy Rob.

I square my shoulders and join the herd of passengers shuffling down the ramp to Harborside Road. Lined with cast-iron lampposts and giant old poplar trees, the street meanders along the waterfront and disappears into a silver mist. I imagine entering that mist and emerging in a new world where men don't have affairs, where two people can rewind time, fall in love again, and not hurt each other, but I know this is impossible. Time moves in one direction. I must keep up the pace toward Auntie's bookstore, although my heels were not made for brick sidewalks and my coat is too thin for the weather.

The town hasn't changed in the year since I last visited. Classic Cycle, Fairport Chiropractic, Island Eye Care. One token business for each human need. If you want a selection from which to choose, you're out of luck. A handwritten Rotary Bake Sale sign flaps in the window of the Fairport Café, where neighbors gather to share gossip and recipes.

I can't remember when I last had time to crack open a cookbook. In L.A., Rob and I subsisted on takeout, a secret that would annoy my mother. She believes every good Bengali daughter should be like my sister, Gita, who excels at preparing curried fish. I barely remember how to boil water. Now that I'll be staying with my parents, I'll have a harder time hiding my flaws.

I set off toward Auntie's bookstore, six blocks north at the water's edge—a three-story Queen Anne Victorian painted in burnt umber and white. As I approach the house, a little girl runs out the front door, crying, followed by her mother.

"But I wanted *Curious George!*" the little girl wails.

". . . next time," her mother says and bundles her into a Volkswagen Beetle.

I stop at the curb in front of the bookstore, my heartbeat kicking up. I'm not prepared for screaming children. And I forgot how large the house is, and how complex—a pattern of bay windows, turrets, and a wraparound porch. Close up, patches of disrepair come into stark relief. The paint is peeling on the railing; a few shingles have come loose on the roof. Auntie should renovate, repaint, and place a neon sign in the window.

I take a deep breath and drag my suitcase up the narrow steps to the back door, which is now the main entrance to the bookstore. A well-worn path leads around the house to the ornate front door facing the waterfront, recalling a bygone era when important guests arrived by sea. Now I doubt anyone important ever crosses the threshold.

As I push open the back door, soft voices float toward me. The words coalesce, then change their minds and drift away. Inside the foyer, I'm submerged in dimness, save the faint orange glow from a Tiffany lamp. I'll add a few bright lights to this entryway.

The heavy door slams behind me, shutting out the world. The lemon scent of furniture polish rises through the dust; the air hangs heavy with the smell of mothballs. I can't survive a month in this stuffiness, among useless antiques and out-of-print titles.

And the clutter. Auntie leaves no surface uncovered. To my left, a dusty Kashmiri carpet hangs on the wall, depicting the tree of life in subtle shades of red and gold. As I step closer, the colors shift to green and yellow. Perhaps the light has changed, or perhaps the Hindu elephant-headed god, Ganesh, is playing a trick on me. He sits to my right, a brass statue waiting to frighten customers away. Auntie should display bestsellers here, not statues.

5

But before I can stop myself, I reach out to rub Ganesh's enormous belly. He will curse me for not kneeling to touch his feet. After all, he is powerful, temperamental, and unpredictable.

"Maybe you could curse Rob, make his penis fall off," I whisper to Ganesh. He does not reply.

I leave my luggage next to him and nearly bump into a man who seems to have materialized from nowhere. I look up into a rugged face, shadowed eyes, dark, windswept hair. A faint blue glow shines behind him, accentuating his silhouette. He's dressed for leisure in a hooded travel jacket, brown cargo pants, and hiking boots. He's carrying a pile of books under one arm. Apparently he has a lot of time for reading.

"That would hurt," he says. His voice resonates—a deep baritone that ripples across my skin. He gives off the scents of pine trees and fresh air.

"What would hurt?" I can't get past him. He's in my way, and he shows no signs of moving.

"Losing the family jewels."

"Oh, you heard what I said." The blood rises in my cheeks.

"Glad I'm not this Rob guy." A ghost of a smile touches his lips. He's mocking me.

"Believe me, if you were Robert, you'd be dead." I try to slip past him and nearly stumble on a snag in the carpet.

He steps aside. "You're in such a hurry."

"I move at regular speed. I'm not on island time."

His gaze is steady, unabashed. "Where are you from?"

"L.A. I'm here to help my aunt . . . temporarily." I need a hot shower, a cup of espresso.

"Your aunt. That lovely lady in the sari."

"One and the same." So she still attracts the attention of younger men. And she still wears saris.

"Beauty must run in the family," he says.

My ears heat up. I'm glad they're hiding beneath my hair. I haven't felt beautiful in a long time. "You're bold, aren't you, Mr.—?"

"Hunt. Connor Hunt. And you must be Jasmine."

"How do you know my name?"

"I heard your aunt talking about you. She made you sound intriguing."

Me, intriguing? I've never been intriguing. "You heard my aunt gossiping about me? What did she say? I need to have a word with her."

"She said you'll be working for her."

"That's it? That's not intriguing."

"She said you were running away."

"Me, running?" My voice rises, and a knot is forming in the back of my neck. "That's none of your business, and I'm not running. Just to set the record straight."

He raises his hand. "No problem there."

"I have a lot of work to catch up on, so if you don't mind, I should find my aunt."

"Do you have time for coffee? Or tea?"

I can't believe this guy. "I won't have time for dating

while I'm here." *Especially not with men like you. Men who come on to strangers. Men like Robert.*

"Who said anything about a date?" He steps closer, and I step back.

"What would you call it then? Do you always come on to women in bookstores?"

"Only to you. I can't change your mind?"

"Not a chance." I want to shove him out the front door. He's exactly like Robert, who probably flirted with every female he encountered. I'm not going this route again. I've become the fortified castle of Jasmine.

He rubs his forefinger across his eyebrow. "I can't lie. I'm disappointed. But I hope to see you later." He slips out the door and disappears into the blustery evening.

Chapter 2

Good riddance.

The nerve of him, making a pass at a stranger. I bet he's got a wife stashed at home, maybe kids, too.

When Robert first met Lauren, did he smile so innocently and ask her on a date? Did he slide the wedding band off his finger, drop it in his pocket? Did he pretend he cared about her?

Men are driven by testosterone. They think they can get any woman they want. But nobody will get me, ever again. I need to call in to the office, make sure the company hasn't canned anyone else. Make sure I have a job to which I can return.

I hang my coat in the hall closet and slip into the cluttered room to my right. I hold up my BlackBerry at all angles. I check down one aisle, then another. No signal.

A loud snoring emanates from the History aisle labeled

WORLD WAR II. A bearded man has fallen asleep in an armchair, a book about battleships facedown on his chest. Amazing how some people have so much time to sleep, to read. Don't they have work to do? E-mails to check?

"Bippy, my dearest niece!" Auntie exclaims behind me in a voice far bigger than her size. She has always called me by my baby nickname.

"Auntie!" I whip around, and she rushes toward me, arms outstretched. She's as spritely as a teenage girl, yet her paper-white hair, deeply wrinkled face, and silver-rimmed bifocals betray her age. Her knitted reindeer sweater clashes with her green chiffon sari. She shows no trace of her mystery illness.

"Why didn't you say you'd arrived?" She envelops me in a hug filled with her particular spicy scent, the scent of Auntie, and a touch of Pond's cold cream. Childhood memories flood back to me, of Auntie making curried cauliflower and the sweet yogurt dessert *mishti doi*; handing me brand-new copies of *Curious George*, *Winnie the Pooh* . . . Did I ever actually read those silly books?

I gaze into her eyes, searching for a hint of what ails her. "I was looking for you. How are you?"

"I'm holding up, thank the gods."

The guy in the armchair snores louder.

A man rushes into the room in a haze of irritation. He's dressed in autumn colors, black hair teased and oiled. He probably spends an hour in front of the mirror every morning, primping and coiffing. He exudes delicate, elegant charm, his features rounded as if sculpted by the weather.

"Ruma, the window display is messed up again, and I am sick of fixing it." He glances at the snoring man and shakes his head. "Weekend warriors are starting early, and it's only Monday."

"Weekend warriors?" I say.

The man glances at me. "The loungers, the sleepers!"

"You don't get too many of those, do you?"

"Where have you been, honey?" He looks me up and down. "Oh, you must be Jasmine."

"Pleased to meet you," I say, wondering what Auntie has told him about me.

"This is Tony," Auntie says. "You'll be working with him while I'm away."

I smile to hide the jumping beans in my gut. "Looking forward to it," I say politely.

Tony shakes my hand so tightly, my bones nearly break. "So you're moving in."

I let go of his hand. "I'm only visiting. I'll be staying with my parents a few blocks away."

Tony's mouth opens into a round O. "Oh, no, you won't. You need to hold down the fort. That means you stay here."

I turn to my aunt. "Is he serious?"

"Of course. That's part of the deal. You must be a care-taker for the house."

"I can't stay. I'll spend the nights at Ma and Dad's, in the guest room. I need a desk for my work, a table. Your attic apartment is too small."

"Ah, but it's the best spot in the house."

"But Ma has the extra bedroom made up. Lots of space there."

"Out of the question. You must be here, in case the toilets act up . . ."

"The toilets?" I'm not a plumber.

". . . or there's a power failure or, gods forbid, a fire."

"A fire?!"

"We've got extinguishers. And we have many evening and early morning events. So you see, you have to stay—"

"Events?" I blink. What events could she possibly host in this remote corner of the world?

"Wednesday morning we've got an author coming to sign her books, quite early—"

"Can't Tony come in?"

"I live in Seattle," Tony says, frowning. "I take the ferry. Usually only on weekdays, but I'll be here this weekend to help you out."

Auntie pats my arm. "You see? Tony is dedicated. Bookselling is a lifestyle, not a job. You don't expect to arrive when the store opens and leave when it closes, do you?" Her eyebrows rise like two silver suspension bridges.

"Actually, I do." My handbag is slipping off my shoulder. I hastily pull up the strap.

Tony is chuckling. I want to slap him.

Auntie waggles a bejeweled forefinger in front of my face. "This is the nature of running the bookstore. Working after hours. Sleeping in the attic, listening to the books breathing at night."

"Books . . . breathing?" I hope not. My aunt needs to clean the rooms, open the windows, install more lights, and order in the new bestsellers.

"Full-time job, nah?" she says.

"But I have a lot of work to do while I'm here, for my real . . . my *other* job, and I'm wondering about the cell phone signal."

"You won't find one here." She gives me a warm smile, then turns to Tony. "She's so busy, you know. She helps people sock away their money for retirement."

"In socially responsible accounts," I say. *And if I don't make a perfect presentation to the Hoffman Company when I return to L.A., I may be out of a job.*

Tony looks me up and down again. "Girl, you know how to dress, but those threads are for the city, not here. You can't wear those heels to work. Your feet will start hurting."

My toes are already sore. "I have a pair of sneakers in my suitcase."

"Then wear them. And you have jeans, I hope?"

"Only one pair."

He rolls his eyes. "You'll be doing a lot of laundry, unless you buy another pair of jeans. You're going to be on your feet all day."

"I thought I might help at the checkout register—"

Tony guffaws. "What rock have you been hiding under?"

"I've been living in the real world."

He throws his head back and laughs. "You call L.A. the real world?"

I bite my lip to keep from spouting an acerbic reply. The snoring man snores louder. A bulb flickers on the ceiling; the floor squeaks; and a cloud of dust wafts by. I break into a fit of sneezing. The next few weeks are going to crawl by at a slug's pace.

Chapter 3

Auntie ushers us back through the hall.

"Check that front display in the parlor," Tony says before veering off toward a back room.

Auntie leads me into the front parlor, where the dust rises like a desert sandstorm. I can barely see through the particles hanging in the air. I have a strong urge to run out the door and dash down the street. I'll leave my suitcase behind; who cares. As long as I have my technology.

"Auntie, have you considered opening the place up, bringing in more light, and while you're at it, more copies of the books that are in high demand? Like the titles I saw on display at the airport—"

"Not again!" Auntie stops in front of a window display, hands on her hips. "What a mess. Ay, Ganesh!"

The books are all used classics by Jane Austen, Charles Dickens, Charlotte Brontë.

"Like right here," I tell her, pointing at the display. "Organizing this. Arranging newer books face out. Maybe typing up your recommendations on little cards—"

"You must get to know my store before you rush into giving advice." She gathers up the old books. Behind us, a slim volume slides off the shelf and lands with a thud on the floor. *Altering Your Living Space.* "Oh, stop your complaining," she says to the book, then throws it back on the shelf.

I follow her into the Classics section, where I help her shelve the books. "So the display in the parlor—"

"Is for newer books."

"Do you classify them by title, or by—?"

"Author. Other questions we get: Do you sell stamps? Do you have a copy machine? Do you have the Internet? No, no, and no."

"But why not? The Internet would draw more customers. And maybe add a little café."

"Restroom is in the hall," she says, ignoring my suggestions. "Then they want to know, do I give them a discount because they are spending so much money? Ay, Ganesh."

"Surely you don't get many people asking questions like that. I mean, your store is so *out of the way*." And the weather is miserable.

"Out of the way! I'm most central in this town. People can't live without my bookstore."

Can't live? She's the queen of overstatement. I follow her

to the Literature section. The dust is thick on the window-sills. She extracts a series of hardcovers, which she arranges in the front window display.

"There, back to normal," she says.

"Do you consult the bestseller lists? I understand the independent bookstores have their own recommendations—"

"This is not just any bookstore. Sometimes I wake up, and everything is moved. Books here, books there—"

"Who moves them? Tony? Customers?"

"Who knows? Someone who wishes the classics were not forgotten. The culprit included a few different authors in this display so I would not know who is to blame for the switch. Now come. I'll show you around. We'll have tea."

I don't have time for tea. I need an espresso. "Does this happen often?" I say, following her down the hall.

"Now and then," Auntie is saying. "This and that. Items left behind. People appearing and disappearing. Men sleeping here all day, what gall." She pats my cheek, her gnarled fingers like dry leaves against my skin. "Speaking of gall, what's happening with that pile of dung you call an ex-husband?"

The word *ex-husband* sends my heart plummeting. "I still have to deal with him, unfortunately. We're selling the condo."

"Could you not keep it for yourself?"

"I can't afford the mortgage on my own." No more sunlight spilling across hardwood floors, cozy meals in the breakfast nook, sunsets viewed with Robert's arms around me. "Don't tell Ma and Dad."

"I won't say a word," Auntie says, hugging me. "But I worry about you."

"I'm okay, except the divorce cleaned me out." I should frame my latest bank statement, highlight the nearly zero balance.

"Do you need money?"

"No, no. I'll be okay. You take care of yourself." A lump rises in my throat. I hug her again, and her warmth banishes my uncertainty.

"You'll forget Robert while you're here. The authors will help you." She points to framed prints on the walls, pen-and-ink drawings of famous authors. Charles Dickens. Laura Ingalls Wilder.

I try not to laugh. My aunt has always been eccentric.

"The authors will help you," she says again. "Their words. That man with the large forehead is Edgar Allan Poe. And of course, there's Jane Austen. This is the only surviving sketch of her, a reproduction."

"She looks so young and plain." I touch the picture, the rough canvas of her cheek. Jane's eyes seem to follow me across the centuries.

"Don't speak ill of the dead." Auntie glances around, as if Jane Austen might jump from a corner. "Come, we'll have some tea."

"I need to check my messages." My fingers are itching to get at the keys of my BlackBerry, to get my netbook booted up.

"There will be plenty of time for that." She leads me

down the hall and makes an abrupt left turn into the children's book room. Of course *she* always has plenty of time—she's living in slow motion on the far edge of civilization.

"The stock markets are closed for today, and I need to check some prices."

"If they're closed, they're closed. They'll be closed all night, nah?"

"I suppose, but—"

"Do you remember this room, Bippy?" Toys litter the carpet; books are piled on a low desk in the corner.

"Vaguely." I shift from foot to foot. My toes are squished in these pumps.

"That desk belonged to E. B. White. He sat there to write all his books. Even *Charlotte's Web*. Not in this house, of course. But at that desk."

"Isn't that something." Next, she'll say the ornate candleholders belonged to Jane Austen.

A pigtailed girl sits cross-legged on the floor, reading *Peter Rabbit*. She glances up, then returns to her book. Behind her, watercolors dance across the wall—Winnie the Pooh, the Hungry Caterpillar, Madeline. I'm surprised I remember those characters.

"Do you remember this?" Auntie hands me a tattered copy of *The Cat in the Hat*.

"Everyone knows Dr. Seuss." I push the book back into her hands.

"Do you remember anything more?"

"More than what?" I tap my cell phone. "If I don't find a signal soon, I could lose a client." *I need this job. At Taylor Investments, I'm walking a tightrope.*

"Your clients can wait. If they really love you, they will not abandon you."

Oh, yes, they will. In a heartbeat. "We've already closed three west coast offices. I have to prove my worth. It's all about money, not love."

"Everything is about love," Auntie says and winks again.

I take a deep breath—let her believe what she wants. She has the luxury. "What's next?"

"The Antiquarian room." She leads me into a stuffy room filled with tall bookshelves. "Look there. That mirror belonged to Dickens."

On the wall, I catch a glimpse of my face in an ornately framed, rectangular mirror. Do I really look so tired and puffy? "Great mirror. Must be worth a fortune, if it really belonged to Dickens." Which I doubt.

"Conventional early Victorian chimney breast mirror, circa the eighteen thirties."

A man clears his throat in the aisle, his face lost in shadow.

"Sorry to disturb you," Auntie says; then she mutters under her breath, "If he wants quiet, he should go to a library."

The man is tall, broad shouldered. For a moment, I'm sure he's Connor Hunt, but when he steps into the light, I see he is someone else. This man is clean-cut, wearing a gray suit.

Auntie leads me back to a small, jam-packed office, where

stacks of files cover her desk. Yellow Post-it Notes stick to every surface. "I've got to clean up this place someday. No time, no time."

I'm not accustomed to working in such a mess. My life is organized, categorized, classified. "I could tidy up for you, get rid of some of this clutter," I say, holding out my hands, palms down. On the desk, mixed in with the files, are useless artifacts that Auntie has accumulated through the years—a lacquered, canoe-shaped pen tray full of brushes and fountain pens; a wooden box full of clips; a flat gray rock; a clear bottle of blue ink and an antique white-quill pen.

"How can I part with Faulkner's rock?" she says, pointing. "And Kipling's wooden box? They're rare treasures worth keeping. Now, come with me." She yanks me out into an open tea room, which hasn't changed in decades. A counter runs along one wall, complete with two burners, and there's a miniature refrigerator, cabinets, armchairs, and couches.

"For my customers," Auntie says. "Keeps them here longer."

Nobody is in here. She needs new couches, not threadbare thrift store castoffs. She needs an espresso machine, books lined up on shelves. She needs to sell designer mugs, bookplates, reading lights.

She pours us two mugs of hot tea from a metal pot and motions to two plush blue armchairs. I choose the one with the saggy middle. Auntie sits across from me, kicks off her flat-soled sandals, and wiggles her gnarled toes. She has painted her toenails in silver polish. She sips from her mug and makes a face, as if the tea tastes bitter. "I'm afraid I'm leaving you with a hot mess. You're so good with numbers. Perhaps you'll stay permanently and straighten everything out."

"I have a job, remember? Big presentation to a potential client, right after I get back to L.A." My career depends on it. I'm single again. And broke. I have to make a future for myself.

"Oh." Auntie's face falls. She pats the arm of her chair. Jewelry clinks on her wrists—a cacophony of gold, silver, and painted Kashmiri bangles.

"You're okay, aren't you?" I ask. "Nothing bad is going to happen to you?"

Auntie pats my hand. "Not to worry, Bippy. Your old auntie will come back right as rain."

"Oh, good." I breathe a sigh of relief. I want to know what's wrong with her, but I won't press. When I push too hard, Auntie closes up like a flower at night. "You'll show me the basics before you go, right?"

"I meant to tell you, I must leave tomorrow morning."

I nearly choke on my tea. "So soon?"

"Tony will help you. Quite a character, isn't he?"

"Tony?"

"And I may be out of touch for a while. I won't have a cellular telephone. I have no idea how those silly contraptions work. Which is fine, since cell phones don't work here, either."

"How will I know you're okay?"

"Don't look so worried." Auntie plays with her bangles. "I must have my heart fixed in India."

"Your heart?" I take her hands in mine. My dearest aunt, who has lived here alone for so long, working hard for everyone else, has an ailing heart. "I didn't know. I'm so sorry."

She holds the teacup against her chest. "I've been so tired. But now, now I'll be well again, and whole."

"You can't be treated here?"

"What must be done must be done in India. I must go home."

"If you're sure."

"Don't tell anyone. This is my secret. I don't want your ma and dad to worry about me."

"But what if—?"

"Nothing will happen to me. You must promise."

I sigh. "Mum's the word. But let me know how you are."

She squeezes my fingers. "First, I must visit family. And then, well . . . I should be ready to return in a month."

I lift her hand and press it to my cheek. "I love you. Please take care of yourself."

She kisses my forehead. "Thank you for coming, for agreeing to help Tony in the store. He's skilled and experienced, but I need your special talent."

I don't have any talent, but I'll help my aunt, as long as she takes care of her heart. "I won't let you down."

"You must try to find some happiness here."

I laugh dryly. "I'll watch over your store. Nobody said anything about happiness."

She gives me an intense look. "You must never stop believing in love. Forget about Robert the dung heap."

"I believe in love for *you*. You'd better get well and come home, so we can find you a good man."

Her eyes twinkle. "Don't worry about me." She gets up and slips her feet back into her sandals. "Now, your ma and baba want you to arrive in time for supper. Let me show you the attic apartment before you go. You'll find magic upstairs."

Chapter 4

Magic, my eye.

The thought of sleeping in Auntie's tiny apartment in mossy, damp darkness gives me chills. Black mold is probably growing on the walls. I'll stay in this creaky old haunted house when hell freezes over or pigs fly, whichever comes last. But I humor my fragile aunt, following her up a wooden staircase in the center of the house. "I forgot how narrow these steps are," I say.

She swipes at cobwebs, her sari gently swishing. "These stairs were originally for the servants. The main staircase in the front of the house—that was for everyone else. Don't you remember?"

"Vaguely. We should stick to the well-lit staircase, don't you think?" I haven't set foot in the bookstore in years. Who has time? During my last visit to the island, Auntie came to see me at my parents' house.

"The main staircase only goes up to the second floor," she says. "My apartment is in the attic. Third floor. You'll be sleeping on top of the world."

"I'll come here in the morning to open the store, and I'll stay in the evening until the last customer leaves. But I'm not sure about sleeping here—"

"Remember, you must immerse yourself in the life of a bookseller. There is no halfway."

I clear my throat. The dust thickens as we climb; the smell of age grows stronger. "I'll hold down the fort. I know you said nobody else will do. But I'm not a bookseller. I'm only going to pretend to be one."

She pivots on her heel, hitching up the sari to reveal her slim calves. Her eyes glint. "There is no pretending, Bippy. You promised to help me."

"And I will, but . . . I don't want to invade your space. By staying in your apartment and all."

"You mean you're afraid of this creaky old house."

"That's not it." But I am afraid. I'm afraid of empty rooms, moaning floorboards, the wind rattling the window-panes at night. I'm already rattled, my insides battered by Robert's betrayal. I'm afraid of my own thoughts, of sleeping on one side of the bed, waking alone. I'm afraid my aunt may not come back.

"Then you'll have no trouble watching over my precious bookstore while I'm in India. If you don't stay here, well, the house becomes cranky. In a manner of speaking." She opens a door into the attic apartment, dimly lit by antique lamps and packed with furniture and books. Everything from the narrow overhead beams to the floors is made of a golden wood. Layer upon layer of age and dust breathe from the rafters. The place is so small, a doll could live here.

"Enchanting, isn't it?" Auntie bustles through the miniature living room and yanks open a wavy glass window. Cool air rushes in, replete with the scents of cedar and damp grass. A few flecks of white paint fall from the sill and land on the hardwood floor.

"The apartment is quaint." I press a finger to my nose. My eyes are tearing up from the dust again—the room swims in a watery haze.

"Those are Hemingway's pencils," she says, pointing to an antique desk in the corner, littered with writing instruments. "John Steinbeck preferred pencils as well." She picks up a yellow fountain pen, holds it carefully between thumb and forefinger. "Mandarin Yellow Parker Duofold used by Colette."

"Quite a collection." I play along, although I doubt any of these items belonged to any famous authors. She probably found them at local garage sales.

"You'll watch over them?"

"Of course." I have no intention of staying overnight, but sure, I'll watch over her things . . . from downstairs.

She shows me the tiny bathroom, in which a gilt-framed mirror hangs above an antique ceramic sink.

"Dickens?" I say.

"Of course not," she scoffs. "Emily Dickinson. Found it on a trip to Massachusetts many moons ago."

"Does the museum know you have it?"

"They would deny it ever belonged to her."

"So how do you know it did?"

"How do you know it didn't?"

I should know better than to press.

Auntie shows me her storybook bedroom. She claims the brass double bed frame belonged to Marcel Proust, who wrote while lying down. The mattress sags in the middle—and she expects me to sleep here, beneath an elaborate spiderweb hanging from the ceiling?

In the tiny kitchen, garlic cloves and onions hang in baskets; various colors of squash and miniature pumpkins are arranged in a bowl.

"Plenty of vegetables for your recipes," Auntie says.

"I don't usually cook, but thanks." I have no idea what to do with raw ingredients that require *preparation*. I don't have time to slice up a squash and watch it bake in the oven for an hour.

"I hope you enjoy my humble abode." Auntie clasps her hands to her chest, a warm smile on her face.

"You'll be back in no time." I turn away from her, toward the window, to hide my worries. Across the water, majestic, snow-capped Mount Rainier rises fourteen thousand feet above the landscape. "You'll come back to this beautiful view."

"Yes, isn't it lovely?" she whispers behind me. But when I turn around, nobody is there. Auntie has already left the room.

Chapter 5

I hurry along Harborside Road toward my parents' house on Fairport Lane. In the biting wind, I pass evening walkers, joggers, and couples strolling arm in arm. They stare into each other's eyes as if they will always remain in love.

I hold my cell phone up at all angles. No signal. Fairport Café is closed early, too. No newspaper stand, no *Wall Street Journal*.

At least I've escaped every foul whiff of Robert. I can keep my eye on Auntie's musty store for a few weeks, clean up the place, no problem.

I'm here, at my parents' Cape Cod–style house perched on the bluff overlooking the bay. Along the walkway to the front door, my mother has planted perennials in terra-cotta pots, and as usual, the lawn is pristine, nearly unnatural in its sharp-edged neatness.

As I raise my hand to knock, Ma opens the front door. She is compact, straight backed, her hair cropped close to her face. Ma rarely wears a sari, preferring beige slacks and printed blouses. Her skin is light, her hair squirrel brown. Warm air wafts out around her and draws me into the pink-tiled foyer. Scents of onion, cumin, and garlic drift through the air. I'm home.

"So Auntie finally let you leave!" Ma says, hugging me.

"She held me under siege, but I escaped."

"I'm glad you're staying here instead of in that dusty old house. I don't know how Ruma can stand the untidiness. Come in. Gita took the ferry over this morning. She's upstairs having a shower. She's been preparing dinner all afternoon."

"She's such a chef," I say, feeling a pang of envy somewhere behind my ribs. Gita, my dear younger sister, knows how to whip up gourmet meals. She knows how to choose the latest fashion and make it all look effortless. I, on the other hand, know how to choose blue suits and ill-fitting pumps that give me blisters. And how to get the top off a gourmet take-out container without damaging my nails.

I peel off my outer layer, remove my shoes, and follow Ma into the living room. The furniture forms a smorgasbord of my parents' travels—folk art from Hawaii, India, Africa.

"I need an Internet connection," I say, trying not to sound stressed.

"In my study, as always." My father shows up with a glass of whiskey in hand. Stooped and gaunt, he seems to have shrunk an inch or two since I last saw him. He has aged in his wrinkled linen pants and shirt, his gray hair mussed.

I hug him tightly, surprised at the emotion welling inside me. I've missed him, too. And my e-mail. "I'll be right back."

I slip down the hall to his messy study. I sign into my account and find 157 new messages since this morning. Ninety-seven are urgent.

Three messages pop up from Robert, directing me to check my voice mail. *Contingent offer on condo, below asking price. Where are you?*

I hadn't told him about my trip. Let him wonder, for once. How gullible I was, sitting up on clear summer nights, waiting for him, believing he simply had to work late.

I type quickly. *I never wanted to move. You drove me out of my home. No way will I accept a dollar below the asking price.*

I delete the message before sending, sit back, and take several deep breaths. I hope the buyers don't rip out my flower garden or remove the stones in my walkway. But I have to let go of the condo. I've got no choice.

"You all right?" Dad asks from the doorway. "We're having supper." He swirls the whiskey in his glass. He is always swirling or twirling something—if not whiskey, then a fork or a straw or an unlit cigar.

"I'm fine." I sign off and follow him into the dining room. We sit at the long oak table, the table my parents have owned since my earliest memories—the table at which I sat through countless meals, where I refused to eat liver and instead fed our cat, Willow, under the table. She died of old age, or maybe the liver killed her.

There is an empty chair next to me, the chair in which Rob used to sit when we came to dinner. Now the space is bare, his green bamboo place mat gone. Ma has laid out the rest of the settings and the good silver cutlery. She is neat, reining in the centrifugal force of my father's messiness. I know without looking that if I open any drawer in the house, its contents will be arranged in compartments, letters held together with rubber bands. I know my mother still keeps the blinds drawn on sunny days, to prevent bleaching of the hardwood floor. Unlike me, she never allows leftovers to accumulate in the back of the refrigerator.

Seated at the head of the table, Dad swirls the ice in his tumbler of whiskey. "Good to have you home. Your sister has some—"

"I thought I heard Jasmine's voice." Gita emerges from the kitchen, her hair still damp from her shower, a plate of basmati rice in hand. I stand, hugging her, avoiding the plate of rice. In her designer pantsuit and colorful jewelry samplers, she is a walking advertisement for her Seattle boutique. Her angular face could grace the cover of *Vogue*.

"How's Dilip?" I ask her. "Is he—?"

"Business trip," Gita says quickly, smiling, as if she's hiding a secret. "He'll be back tomorrow. If he's not, I'm leaving him."

Mom gasps. "Gita! What about, you know?"

Gita holds up her hand. "Wait, Ma! When I'm ready, I'll tell her."

"Tell me what?" I say.

"Sit down and relax first." Gita smiles a bit too brightly, motioning me back into my chair. I can't get comfortable. The wood is hard and cold.

"Jasmine looks tired, doesn't she?" Ma says. Translation: *Jasmine works too much. She needs to spend more time with her family.* My mother often speaks sideways, to my sister, when she means to admonish me instead.

Gita sits across from us. "So Jasmine, how are you holding up? What's going on with that jerk? Is everything all settled or is Robert still being an asshole?"

Ma gasps. "Gita! Watch your language."

Gita rolls her eyes. "Okay, is he still being a shithead? You must be so glad to be free of him."

Ma frowns.

I smile, although my heart is splintering. "I'm free. I'm doing . . . great." Gita means well, but she has no idea what it's like to pack your husband's belongings into boxes, to find reminders of him left behind—a dry cleaning receipt, a grocery list scrawled in his slanted handwriting, half a bottle of his favorite wine.

Mom lets out an audible breath. "Come, let's eat! We're all hungry."

Gita has conjured a spread of fragrant mango chutney, fish curry, and *aloo gobi*, my favorite. Of all the Bengali dishes she has mastered, I most relish the curried potato and cauliflower. The complex scent swirls through the air in a medley of coriander, garlic, ginger, onion, green chiles, and turmeric. My mouth waters, reminding me that I can still enjoy these simple pleasures.

The subtle aromas carry me back to India, to the dust and noise of Kolkata, the crowds, the rustle of saris. I should return to the country of my birth, although I haven't visited in nearly a decade. Perhaps I could find a better mate there—the loyal, elusive Bengali husband. But I doubt he exists anywhere except in my mother's imagination.

She piles food on the plates, while Dad swirls his whiskey and Gita shovels mouthfuls of rice and curry into her mouth. She is not a delicate eater.

"So when are you going to tell me your news, Gita?" I ask. The water in my glass is lukewarm.

There's a sudden silence.

"Dilip and I are getting married," Gita says finally, with her mouth full.

Dad clinks his glass against his plate. "Finally, after all this time."

"Dad! We've only been living together for a year." Gita's top lip trembles, the way it does when she is holding back anger.

"A year!" Dad laughs. "Your mother and I had how many dates together?"

"Three," Ma says. "And two were chaperoned by our parents."

Gita stabs her fish with her fork. "Times have changed. People live together all the time."

Ma straightens her napkin next to her plate. Her eyes are bright. "We're busy with all the plans. So much to be done." She looks at me carefully, as if seeking permission to get excited about the wedding. "Gita and Dilip would like to be married here—"

"On the island, at Island Church," Gita cuts in. "We're making up a guest list. I hope I don't forget anyone. The reception will be out in the park, overlooking the water. We're combining East and West. I might wear a sari, if I can find a good one. Jasmine, you must come sari shopping with Ma and me."

The mound of food on my plate has grown impossibly large. I've lost my appetite. "When did you decide all this?"

Gita glances at Ma. "A few days ago. We waited to tell you. We know you're going through a lot. Auntie doesn't know yet, either. You are happy for me, right?"

"Of course I'm happy for you." But I'm not sure whether the tears in my eyes are out of happiness for her or misery for myself. "Congratulations, Gita. This is wonderful news."

Gita and Ma trade glances again.

"Thanks," Gita says.

I dab at my mouth with my napkin. "When is this . . . wedding going to happen?"

"April twentieth," Gita says. "Auspicious date, according to Dilip's family astrologer."

I can't believe this. "He has an astrologer?"

Ma frowns at me. "We may not believe in such things, but we honor tradition."

She means I didn't honor tradition when I married Robert in a secular Western ceremony, and look what happened.

I ignore Ma's sour expression and turn toward Gita. "What are you going to do, after you're married? Are you still going to run the boutique?"

"Of course! In this economy, people are flocking to the used clothing racks."

Dad twirls his fork. "We'll see how long that lasts. And Jasmine, how long will your visit last?"

"Until Auntie comes back from India."

"Why don't you stay longer?" he asks gently.

"Auntie's coming back. I have a presentation at work."

Mom turns to me. "I suppose it's difficult to keep up with everything these days."

"I'm keeping up just fine."

She attacks her potatoes with her fork. "Have you started seeing anyone? A new boyfriend?"

Gita drops her fork on her plate. "Ma, it's way too soon for that."

"I'm not dating," I say. "I'll have my hands full at Auntie's." I think of Connor Hunt. No way am I going to mention my encounter with him. And anyway, a stranger hitting on you in the bookstore does not constitute dating.

"Yes, your hands will be full," Ma says. "Be careful in that rickety house."

"I can handle it." I laugh, a bit nervously.

"Auntie has always believed the bookstore is haunted," Gita says. "You'd better watch out." She points her fork at me. Grains of rice fly off and hit the table.

"The house is not haunted," I say. "It's just . . . old."

Ma wipes the rice off the table with a napkin. "Ruma has always been peculiar, believing in ghosts and such. Keep your feet firmly planted in reality, and you'll be fine."

But my feet are not planted anywhere. I feel uncertain, ephemeral. I have to hold tight to my water glass, or I might float away.

Chapter 6

"Do you have time to talk?" Gita stands at the threshold of the upstairs guest room. I'm sitting on the bed with my laptop propped on my thighs.

I look up, pulling the reading glasses down my nose. "If it won't take too long." I couldn't bear to discuss the minutiae of her wedding plans. In the radiant heat of her excitement, I might burn to ash.

Gita's face contorts, as if she has developed a terrible pain in an unspecified part of her body. "I'll just, uh, head off to bed then."

I take off the glasses, motion her to come in. "I'm sorry. Let's talk." I reluctantly roll up the green bar reports, which were laid out across the bed.

Gita steps inside, tiptoeing as if trying not to disturb the carpet. "Do you ever miss our old place? The giant cedar tree in the backyard, the one with the low branches? I miss climbing that tree and looking across the fence into the neighbor's backyard."

I barely remember our rambler on the other side of town, near a forest trail. "I don't really think about it. I haven't thought about that cedar tree in a long time. . . . I guess I've been too busy working."

"You don't have to work so hard, day and night," Gita says.

"Yes, I do. First of all, I need the money. But second, work keeps me sane."

She sits next to me on the bed. "I hope you can take time off to be my maid of honor at the wedding."

The oxygen ebbs from my lungs. At my wedding, Gita stood beside me in a yellow silk dress. She watched Robert slip the ring on my finger, hold my hand while he recited his vows to love and cherish me forever. "Bengali ceremonies don't have maids of honor."

"Maybe not, but I want you there. And when Ma and I go sari shopping on Friday, will you come? Maybe you'll find a sari for yourself."

I make a face. "You know I'm not crazy about wearing a sari." I don't have time to wrap myself in several yards of silk fabric, tuck the pleats in at the waist, and then try to power walk to work. Saris have been known to fall off at inopportune moments, and besides, they're formal wear, quintessentially Indian. They're just not . . . me.

Gita is glowing. "Do this for me? I'm so excited. I've wanted this for so long!"

"Can't you order a sari from India?"

"Why do that when we have boutiques here? But we might also get some saris from India. And who knows, maybe I'll have another ceremony there. Dilip and I have talked about that."

"Will any of his relatives be flying in from Kolkata?"

"Yes, of course. His grandparents and a couple of cousins." She plays with the tassels on the bedcover. "I hate rattling around in that house while he's gone. When I'm alone, half of me is missing."

My internal organs seem to shrivel. Love is so easy for Gita. She and Dilip have always sailed along, gaga in love, drooling over each other. "Is he away a lot these days?"

"He works hard. They've got him opening offices in Bulgaria and Bangalore. Next it will be China."

"Why don't you go with him?"

"I can't leave the shop for that long."

"Does he stay in touch when he's away? I mean, can you keep tabs on him?"

She lets go of the tassels. "He calls me every night. Sometimes several times a day."

"Well, good for him."

She gives me a sharp look. "I can't help it if he's a good guy. He cares about me. He loves me."

It hurts hearing this. Robert used to care about me, too. Now he cares about Lauren. "Sure he does. All men love women—as many as they can get."

"Since when did you become so bitter? Don't take it out

on me just because Robert turned out to be such a pig. Dilip is not Robert. And you're not yourself anymore."

"Nope, I'm not," I say flatly, refusing to show any pain over her words. "Robert leached all the self out of me."

"You don't have to be so mean." She busies herself fluffing the pillows. "You're just like Ma and Dad. So pessimistic, always thinking the worst, giving me advice as if I'm a child. Dad still thinks I might become a cardiac surgeon when I grow up. He thinks I'm playing dress-up at the boutique. Wake up, Dad. Hello. I'm never going to cut open anyone's rib cage."

"Dad wanted me to be a pediatrician." I type an e-mail to Robert as I'm talking, a polite refusal of the lowball offer on the condo. I hit the Send button. "Can you imagine?"

"And me a surgeon!" Gita hugs a pillow to her chest.

"Can you picture it? You doing open-heart surgery and me prescribing penicillin to snotty-nosed kids?"

"Kids aren't so bad." Gita frowns. "I wouldn't mind having a few kids someday. . . ."

"Why? If you get divorced, they'll be just another part of the battle."

"Who says there will be any divorce?"

"Statistics. Most first marriages end in divorce."

"You're worse than bitter. You're— I don't know what! Robert really did a number on you, didn't he? Don't you still believe in love? Can't you believe in it for my sake?"

A familiar ache settles beneath my ribs. I gaze out the window at the rough water, lit by a pale, indifferent moon.

No matter what goes on below, the moon still travels across the sky. Cities burn; wars rage; civilizations topple and disappear. Lonely women cry. And yet that damned moon keeps rising and falling. The water keeps flowing in the sea—and Robert keeps living without me.

I take a deep breath, and my insides fall like an elevator full of stones. "Honestly, Gita, I don't know what I believe in anymore."

Chapter 7

In the morning, after a quick breakfast of cereal and two cups of extra-strong coffee, I bundle up, shove files into my briefcase, sling my handbag over my shoulder, and head for the front door. All for the love of Auntie Ruma.

"Wait. I made you lunch." Ma rushes up, waving a paper bag, and suddenly I'm a kid again, heading off to school. I have the same sinking feeling—as if I'm about to take a test, and I forgot to study.

"Thanks, Ma. You didn't have to do that. I was going to buy my lunch."

"Why waste your money? Everything is overpriced at Island Market. No competition." She stuffs the paper bag into my gigantic handbag. "What on earth have you got in there? You're carrying all that stuff to the bookstore?"

"I've got some work I need to get done. I need to make a few calls on the way. Where can I get a cell phone signal?"

"Best chance is along the waterfront, before you round the bend into town. Watch out for the waves. They sneak up on you."

"See you later, Ma." Waves, my eye. My mother loves to warn me about the dangers in life. My plane might crash. Auntie's house will go up in flames. I'll trip, crack my head open, and end up in a coma. And now errant ocean waves will drown me.

But I can get a good calf workout in the sand, so I make for the beach. I spot pink cockleshells, white clamshells, blue and red chunks of volcanic rock. I can't stop to pick them up. I've got too much weight on my shoulders.

A gaggle of cormorants chatters on the waves. Seagulls hover above, calling in their high-pitched voices. I speed walk past a couple of early risers—an elderly woman and man strolling hand in hand. They look so happy, like two pieces of a puzzle that fit perfectly together.

My answer to melancholy—technology. I'm on the phone, finally checking my messages. Robert's voice still makes my heart jump, a reflex reaction to the sound of his smooth tenor, the faint hint of a Texas accent. *Heeeyyy, Jasmine.*

As I listen further, I clench my jaw. Robert's tone is lightweight, unencumbered by guilt or regret. I wish he would grovel at my feet, so I could enjoy the pleasure of rejecting him. But he never comes crawling back to me. *I need to ask you a favor,* he says. The rest of the message is garbled.

I return his call, and his cell phone dumps me into voice mail. *You've reached the disembodied voice of Robert Mahaffey. You know what to do.*

I know what to do, and I would do it, if it weren't illegal. If I wouldn't end up in jail for life.

"The answer is no," I say. "No to the lowball offer on the condo." I hang up, blink tears from my eyes, and focus on returning calls from clients. I pitch portfolios, selling my skills as morning sunlight breathes across the sky. Cold, salty air whips against my face. In my windbreaker, jeans, and running shoes, I barely ward off numbness. I follow the line of the surf toward town.

". . . choose our socially responsible growth fund," I'm saying, and then I scream as an icy wave rushes up to my thighs. "Oh, I have to call you back!"

I run up the beach, lifting my feet like a prancing horse to get out of the water. I'm soaked, and I'm already more than halfway to the bookstore. No turning back now. By the time I reach Auntie's doorstep, I'm on the verge of hypothermia.

Inside, the house is quiet and warm. The spicy scent of chai wafts down the hall, mixed with the usual dust and mothball odors. I'm shivering, my teeth chattering. "Auntie, hello! Help!"

Auntie rushes down the hall in a new clashing outfit—blue sari and purple striped sweater. "Bippy, did you fall in the sea?"

"Nearly." I unload my technology in the parlor. "My feet are numb."

"Come, come—we'll put your clothes in the dryer and

your shoes in front of the heater. I've got some pants for you to wear in the meantime." She leads me to the laundry room, next to the office, hands me a towel, and rushes away.

I peel off my wet jeans, underpants, and socks, shove them in the dryer, and wrap a towel around my waist. Now what? I'm standing here half-naked, with no cell phone signal and no prospects for a happy life.

Auntie returns with a pair of baggy purple polyester pants with an elastic waist; orange socks; and giant fluffy slippers in the shape of rabbits, complete with two ears growing up from each foot. I put on the clothes. I look like a giant grape. I'm glad Auntie didn't bring a pair of her panties. I hope my jeans dry in record time.

"You look nice and warm now." She steps back and grins. "Perhaps you'll wear this to Gita's wedding!"

"So Ma told you."

"She called me early this morning. What wonderful news!"

"The best news I've heard in years."

Auntie pats my shoulder. "Stop making such a long face. You mustn't stop believing in love, nah?" She glances at her watch. "I've got more packing to do upstairs before the store opens."

"The front door is already open."

"For early risers who like to come in and have tea or coffee before work." She heads for the stairs.

"So technically, you're open?"

"Oh, I suppose, but not really. I'll be finished soon and come right back down."

"But what about showing me—?"

"I'll be down again soon. Make yourself at home."

She disappears. Fine, leave me here.

I head for the parlor to retrieve my technology and nearly bump headlong into . . . Connor Hunt.

My face flushes. I gaze down at my baggy purple pants, my giant rabbit slippers. How did he get in here? Through the door, of course. But I didn't see him come in. He's not supposed to be here. Does he ever wear anything other than cargo pants, travel jacket, and hiking boots? Does he have a job, or does he spend his life reading in dusty old bookstores? "What are you doing here, Mr. Hunt?"

"Research." He shoves a book back onto the Fun New Arrivals shelf: *101 Uses for an Old Farm Tractor*.

"You have an old farm tractor?" I wish I could hide behind a bookshelf. I hope he can't tell that I'm going commando.

"Not exactly." He gazes at my slacks, the rabbit slippers, and smiles. "But the title looked . . . intriguing."

"The book is obscure. This one, too." I grab *Across Europe by Kangaroo*. "Who on earth would travel this way?"

"Someone adventurous?" He smiles. His eyes look darker today, more intense. "But this family took a van across Europe, not a kangaroo."

"False advertising." A book falls on its side on the shelf, making a dull clapping sound. I pick up the book—*Be Bold with Bananas* by Crescent Books. "Look at this picture. Makes me never want to eat another banana. Are they sliced or glazed? And what are those red things? Who buys this kind of book?"

Connor peers closely at the cover image. "Someone impulsive? Someone who departs from the ordinary?"

I put the book back on the shelf. "A bookstore is a business. My aunt needs to pay more attention to turning a profit, not departing from the ordinary."

"Isn't reading all about departing from the ordinary?" He's staring at me, his gaze pinning me again.

"Sure, if you've got time for it. . . ."

"That's it? You have no interest in unusual book titles? I'm doing research on unusual tomes."

"I'm sure my aunt has many more in other rooms as well. You're here early, doing your . . . research."

He glances at his watch, an old silver chronograph with a leather strap. "Is there a law against showing up when the store opens?"

"I'm not sure if the store is open yet . . . technically."

"I like to get here before the crowds descend."

What crowds? "Well," I say, exhaling, "I'll go and find my aunt."

"Wait, not so fast. You're so quick to reject me." He touches my arm, sending a peculiar electric wave through my body.

I pull away, startled. "I have work to do, and I don't know anything about you."

"I'm a doctor. I used to live on the island, many years ago. I traveled quite a bit, and now I'm back, visiting. I'm thinking of settling here again. What else do you want to know?" His gaze follows my rabbit slippers up past the purple pants to my black turtleneck sweater, and I feel, somehow, as though he has magically removed every piece of my clothing.

"So, you're a doctor?" I say quickly, annoyed. "What kind of doctor?"

"Internal medicine. And you? What do you do?"

My fingers are slowly thawing. I need to buy gloves. "I'm an investment manager."

I can't read the expression in his eyes—assessing, hungry, critical? "You don't look like one."

"And you don't look like a doctor."

"I don't normally dress this way."

"Me, either. I had a run-in with a rogue wave on the way here."

"I'm glad you survived."

I glance down at Auntie's orange socks, the rabbit ears. "I didn't know my aunt had these slippers. Better than pumps, I guess. More comfortable."

"That's why I like this place," Connor says. "The absence of pumps. Not a single pair on the whole island. I believe the dearth of shoe stores is what keeps this place so quiet and rural. Stops people from moving here. That's my theory."

"It would certainly keep my ex-husband away."

One eyebrow rises. That piercing gaze again, a doctor's gaze. I wonder if he notices the pulse in my neck. "Your ex liked shoes?"

"Had way too many of them. Armani, Rockport, Ferragamo. He was a shoe junkie." I'm telling Connor Hunt too much.

"So you're single now, free of all those shoes. Have coffee with me."

"We're back to that. I have a bookstore to run."

"And you don't date because your bastard ex-husband screwed you and now you can't ever fall in love."

"You must be a mind reader." I focus on the banana book. "It doesn't matter, either way. I'm planning to be alone from now on."

"But I can tell you're an optimist at heart."

"I know you mean well, Dr. Hunt—"

"Call me Connor."

"Connor. I've been through a lot, and I need some quiet time in this store." My voice is a wavering thread. I don't want to date anyone. I'm not ready for that.

"I doubt this store is going to be quiet," he says.

"It has been so far."

"You showed up in the evening—I bet evenings are slower, when people go home for dinner."

My heart skips a few beats. "Tony and I will handle whatever comes."

"You could take a break."

"You're persistent, aren't you?"

He grins. "I don't like to give up."

"It was good to see you again," I say in a neutral voice. "But I'm really sorry, I can't go out with anyone right now. I hope you understand." I'm crossing the room, on my way out to the hall, when the books begin to fall.

Chapter 8

The banana book tips over again, setting off a cascade of falling tomes like dusty dominoes. A hardcover tumbles at my feet, a book of poems by Emily Dickinson, open to a telling page: *Heart, we will forget him! / You and I, to-night!* . . .

I close the book and shove it back on the shelf. "I hope my aunt has earthquake insurance."

Connor rubs his finger across his eyebrow, as if this will help him think. "Not an earthquake. The floor isn't shaking."

"Auntie needs to do a better job of securing these shelves, then." Another book topples onto the carpet, this one a Neruda gift book open to a bright page and the illuminated words . . . *struggling and hoping, / we touch the sea / hoping* . . . A shiver runs through me. I shelve and straighten the books. "Why she keeps silly titles so prominently displayed, I'll never know. Who buys these books?"

"People like me."

"You're strange." I stride to the door, but it slams closed in front of me. I step back, my throat dry.

You have to live, a voice whispers close to my ear. I whip around. "Stop whispering."

"I didn't say a thing." He holds up his hands.

"Who else could it be?" A chill ripples across my skin.

And this maiden she lived with no other thought / Than to love and be loved by me.

"Why are you quoting Edgar Allan Poe?" I say. How do I know the quote came from Poe? "I'm not here to love anyone."

"I didn't say you were." Connor's eyebrows rise.

I shake my head. "He wrote that, didn't he? Poe?"

"Wrote what?"

I'm going insane. "I have to get out of here."

Connor is beside me. "Are you all right?"

"I'm fine." I rattle the knob, but the door won't budge. "We're locked in."

"Let me try." He pulls and turns the doorknob, to no avail.

"Try again." Connor and I both try to open the door. No luck.

"Looks like we'll have to climb out the window," he says.

"I think they're painted shut in this room."

"Then we're trapped in here forever." Connor's grinning, as if the idea isn't so bad.

"This isn't funny."

He glances at my pants, my shoes, the door, and laughs. "I'm sorry, but it is. Let's have coffee and discuss it."

"I don't think so." I twist and rattle and yank the knob, but the door doesn't budge.

It's only coffee, he whispers.

"Okay, okay," I say.

"Okay what?"

"Fine, coffee. But it's not a date. I don't date."

Connor breaks into a dashing smile. "Hey, that's great. Friday night? Around eight o'clock?"

"Okay, okay. Fine." I turn the knob, and magically, the door swings open, setting us free.

Chapter 9

I rush up the stairs and crash headlong into Auntie. She drops a pile of books. They clatter down the stairs. "Bippy, you look pale."

"The wind must have slammed the door in the parlor. I agreed to a date with that man, Connor Hunt. . . ."

"What man, where? What door?"

"Here." I pick up the books, lead Auntie down to the parlor. The door is wide open. Connor is gone, again.

"There was a man in here?" Auntie says. "Splendid. You're going on a date."

"It's not a date. I didn't mean to say date. He kept asking."

"I've heard of this Connor Hunt, but I can't remember where. No need to worry. Enjoy yourself." She rattles the knob. "See, this door does not lock. There is no lock at all."

"But—"

"Look." She shows me the smooth knob, opens and shuts the door.

"I couldn't open it."

Her brows furrow. She steers me back to the tea room. "Sit, take deep breaths. I'll make you some tea."

Tea, her answer to everything. "I'll tell him I can't have coffee with him, next time he stops in," I say, rubbing my temples. "I don't know what got into me. I made a mistake. He said he was doing research on tractors or bananas. Or maybe kangaroos. He's a doctor, too. How does he find time to hang around here? I can't go out with him."

Auntie sits across from me, takes my hands in hers. "Bippy, you're divorced, not dead."

I sigh. "Sometimes I feel . . . well, dead."

"You like this man?"

"He's annoying. I've seen him twice since I arrived . . . and both times, he asked me out."

Her eyes twinkle. "Why not ride the wave, go with the flow. Isn't that what people say?"

I rub my temples. Fatigue seeps into my bones, and the day is still young. "Okay, I give up."

"We haven't much time. Come. Let me show you the shop." She gives me a perfunctory tour of the computer system and checkout register. I try to memorize the keystrokes, but I'm a tad distracted.

"You're staying here tonight, nah?" Auntie says. "But you haven't brought your luggage."

"I couldn't drag it along the beach," I say quickly. "I

wanted to take the scenic route this morning. Ma and Dad will bring my stuff later on." I feel terrible about lying to her.

"I see. *Acha.*" Her face relaxes. "Goodness knows what would happen otherwise."

"I know—the house gets cranky." All the more reason to stay with my parents.

In half an hour, I'm back in my regular clothes and we're dragging Auntie's two giant suitcases down the stairs and out the front door. My family has arrived. They all step out of the car—Gita in a designer trench coat and heels, Ma and Dad more conservatively dressed. Dad grabs both of Auntie's suitcases and drops them in the trunk.

Ma purses her lips, her way of disapproving of her elder sister's adventures in India. If only she knew the real reason for Auntie's trip. The two sisters are so different—Ma tight and controlled, Auntie flowing and flighty. Only their luminous eyes and rounded chins betray the family resemblance. Auntie makes the first move, wrapping her arms around Ma. Ma concedes, then steps away. "Be good," she says. "No craziness."

"I'll be crazier than usual," Auntie says, winking.

"Keep an eye on your passport, and watch out for suicide bombers," Ma says. So her warnings aren't reserved for me. She doles them out freely.

"Stop worrying all the time. I'll be fine," Auntie says.

"Have you packed the gifts?" Ma says.

"Why do you think I have two suitcases?" Auntie points to the trunk. "Chocolate, shampoo, ballpoint pens, clothes, books, perfume, soap."

Gita hops up and down, shivering. "You're going to have a great time, Auntie. Live it up. Don't forget to bring me—"

"You'll have a most beautiful wedding sari," Auntie says.

"And *kurtas* and *chappals*. I want *kajal* and sandalwood oil and turmeric—"

"I shall bring you an entire bazaar."

"Now you're talking," Gita says.

I stand back, away from the wedding excitement. If Gita knew about Auntie's heart problems, she would not make such demands.

"Have you brought Bippy's luggage?" Auntie asks.

I give Ma a *help me* look. I hold my breath.

Ma nods. "Ah, yes—we'll bring it over later on. No room in the car right now."

I let out my breath.

"Good. She must stay here," Auntie says.

"Just come back healthy," I say. "One month." I give her one last hug. I try to memorize the smell of Pond's cold cream and the parchmentlike feel of her skin.

She pats my cheek one last time before getting into the passenger seat of the car. She shuts the door, and Dad reaches over her to pull the seat belt across her lap.

Ma and Gita pile into the backseat, Ma giving me a quick, questioning look. I shrug, then wave and back up toward the house.

Auntie opens the window. "Wait, Bippy. Come here. I nearly forgot."

I rush to her side. She beckons me close, whispers in my ear. "Remember to have fun, Bippy!"

I squeeze her shoulder and smile. "Fly safely."

Dad taps the steering wheel. "We're going to be late!"

"You must take care," Auntie whispers. "Enjoy the moments while you have them."

I wave her off. "Don't worry about me. You get well."

Dad starts up the car, and a plume of exhaust rises from the tailpipe. "We have to go."

"I'll call you," Auntie says.

I step back onto the sidewalk, arms crossed over my chest as Dad pulls the car away from the curb. As my family disappears around the corner, I'm suddenly alone with the bookstore, the rain, and the rising windstorm.

I'm in way over my head.

Chapter 10

In Auntie's messy office, I tackle the stack of paperwork on her desk. She has many unpaid bills and unsent invoices. She's managed to run this business smoothly for years. Her illness must be distracting her, or the down economy is affecting her bottom line.

When Tony arrives, he gives me a perfunctory nod and checks the answering machine. He's dressed in various shades of evening—deep turquoise and black and gray—and sips espresso from a paper cup from Fairport Café. As he listens to the messages from customers, he jots notes, then looks around, shaking his head, hands on his hips. "I try to organize this place. Never makes any difference. Go figure."

I wave a Puget Sound Energy bill. "Should I pay these? Does she have a checkbook?"

Tony snatches the bill from my hand. "Oh, girl, you don't want to go there. I'll pay these. She asked me to."

"Then what does she want me to do?"

Tony makes a grand gesture with his arm. "Take care of the store. Get out there."

"But nobody's here yet. I'm better with numbers. I could balance her accounts. I'm sure there are more bills to pay, invoices to check—"

"And a bookstore to run. I'll show you. Come with me."

Reluctantly, I follow him out into the hall. I spend the next hour helping him unpack boxes of books, shelve titles, rearrange displays.

"Don't put this up front," he says, grabbing a hardcover thriller, *Don't Look Now*, from the windowsill in the parlor.

"But it's new. I saw this title in the airport. Don't you have more copies?"

"We're not a chain store," he says, brandishing an old thriller with a tattered cover. "We provide an alternative, other possibilities."

"Fine. Since you know so much about making the bookstore turn a spectacular profit, I'll leave you to it. I have better things to do."

"I'm sure you do."

I find a broom and a feather duster in a hall closet and set to work wiping every grimy surface. Tony comes up to me in the Antiquarian room and laughs. "You don't expect your efforts to help, do you?"

"A clean shop is a lucrative shop." I try to open the window, but it's painted shut.

Tony keeps shaking his head, his sprayed hair remaining in place. "You don't get it, do you? This store is special. You can't force your will upon it."

"I can force anything I want." I yank on the window again. No luck. "Does my aunt have tools? A screwdriver or something I can use to pry the window open?"

A cracking sound pierces the air. The window pops open a few inches, letting in a blast of fresh air.

"There you go," Tony says, rubbing the palms of his hands together. "Air, all you want."

"How did that happen? There must be a touchy spring."

"Yeah, that must be it." He walks away, shaking his head. "Air, she says. 'A clean shop is a lucrative shop.'"

The rooms are beginning to look half decent, slightly less cluttered, but no matter how hard I work, the bigger the task seems to become.

Throughout the morning, a smattering of customers drifts in and out. A few people pop in to pick up books they've ordered.

"My aunt needs to diversify," I say, wiping down the ornate ceramic mantelpiece in the children's book room. Tony is shelving a stack of picture books. "She should carry soap, candles, handbags, cheaper new paperbacks, like the ones they have in the grocery store. To bring in more customers."

"This isn't a grocery store. Take a look around."

"She needs to come into the twenty-first century, make a modern niche for herself—"

"She already has a niche." Tony runs to answer the ringing phone. "Drop shipment on the fifteenth book," he says into the receiver. "The whole order was supposed to arrive today!" He yells into the phone for a few minutes, then hangs up in a huff.

"You don't want me to improve on anything," I tell him.

"Use your intuitive sense." Tony points a finger at his chest. "Your heart."

"I leave that to Auntie. I have another idea: she could expand—buy the business next door and turn it into a bookstore café."

"We already have a tea room. Didn't you see it?"

"But that room can't compete with the Fairport Café—"

"She's not trying to compete. Okay, watch and learn. Look, there's a live one."

A young bald man has stepped inside the store, shaking his umbrella. Tony strides up to the man and smiles. "How can I help you today?"

"I'm looking for a coffee table book about garden cottages," the man says in a reedy voice. He's in a black trench coat, sleek with water.

I step forward. "We carry many of those." Even I know what a coffee table book is.

The man looks at me blankly, as if I'm invisible and the air has spoken to him. "Built with green materials?"

"The books?" I say. The heat rises in my neck.

The man makes an irritated sound. "Cottages. Built with sustainable materials, energy efficient."

"There's no such thing as an actual coffee table book," Tony says, motioning the man to follow him. "The publishers don't define their books that way. But I'll show you what we've got."

I listen to Tony's smooth voice recede down the hall, as he leads the man to the Home and Garden section. Fine, if Tony is so good at his job, he can do without me for a moment. I'll search for a cell phone signal again. I hold up my BlackBerry in desperate hope, carry it down every aisle in every room, and somehow end up in the Sexuality section, where a woman is furtively sifting through books about female arousal.

I hurry to the next room, my face flushed. I'm glad she didn't ask me for help. That was a close call. In the next aisle over, a little girl begs her father for a fairy book. "This one, please, please. It's only seven dollars."

"Oh, honey, no," her father says, distracted. "That's a waste of money."

The little girl says, "How many packets of cigarettes would that buy, Daddy?"

Silence, except for faint laughter coming from the next room. The father takes the book up to the register. Big surprise—three customers line up ahead of him, tattered old books in their arms. What on earth did they find that interests them?

Every chance I get, I run out to check voice mail, where I've found a blip of a signal five blocks down and two blocks over.

Robert has not called back. He can't sell the condo without me. I need to sign the papers. I haven't agreed to anything.

In the late afternoon, an elderly man, hunched and stiff, slips into the children's book room. He checks through the picture books. Dr. Seuss, animal books . . .

"Can you help me?" he whispers, then looks around. "Ruma always helps me."

"Books for the children in your life?" I say. Tony is in another room, helping someone else.

The man blushes and nods.

"What kind of book are you looking for?" I haven't read a picture book in decades. Outside, the rain is falling steadily.

"Easy ones," he whispers.

"For a girl or a boy?"

"Boy."

"How old is he?"

The man scratches his chin with a thick forefinger and thumb, his nails worn down. "I have trouble keeping track."

A book falls with a thud, one aisle over. A voice whispers, *He does not want it for a boy, he does not want it for a toy. . . .*

"Excuse me? Hello?" I turn the corner, but nobody's there. I return to the man.

"Are you looking for books for . . . *yourself*?" I say. I don't mean to sound—or look—incredulous, but I can't help it. The man must have just learned to read. He must be sixty years old.

His face reddens in blotches. He tosses his book on the table and hurries toward the exit. I run after him. "Sir, wait!" But he leaves in a whirlwind of shame.

"What was that all about?" Tony asks behind me. He peers out the window. "What did you say to him?"

"I asked if the picture books were for him."

"Brava, Jasmine. Score." Tony rolls his eyes.

"The poor man. Should I go after him?"

"Let him go. He'll be back."

But the man does not return. I wish I'd caught his name.

My eyes are itchy from dust, and I'm shivering. The heating system must be on the blink. I close the two open windows, which both popped open on their own, after I fiddled with them.

In the evening, I'm about to close the store, when a slim, tanned woman in a double-breasted Burberry raincoat rushes in, cheeks flushed. She's bony and compact, no part of her wasted. "Hello, Jasmine. I'm Lucia Peleran. *Doctor* Lucia Peleran. Welcome back to Fairport. Is the town the way you remember it?"

I step back and smile. How does she know who I am? "My aunt must have told you about me."

"We're *delighted* to have you back." She gazes closely at my face, so I can smell the faint odor of peppermint on her breath. "If you ever need your back adjusted, you pop right on down to Fairport Chiropractic, and I'll get you fixed right up. You look like you might be out of alignment."

I roll my shoulders and turn my head from side to side. "Nope, I feel just fine."

Her penciled eyebrows pull together. "No kinks? I would think a woman in your situation might have a few knots."

"In my situation?" My stomach tightens. What does she know?

She waves a bony hand, her fingers like the bare twigs on a leafless shrub. "We've all been there, honey, believe me. Just about every woman in this town."

"Been where?" I've been shoved into an unwelcome spotlight.

She leans in close. "I went on a terrible date right after *my* divorce, as well. He wanted to get me into bed. And I realized that it was too soon."

"Excuse me," I say, clenching my hands. "I'm not interested in discussing my personal life."

She keeps right on going. "I needed to take care of myself, go to a spa, sit in a hot tub. An adjustment is what you need—"

"I'm absolutely fine. I've been alone for nearly a year." I told Auntie about my one disastrous attempt to go out on a blind date soon after the separation—a setup orchestrated by my best friend, Carol. I wore a red dress that caught in the car door. I burst into tears before we even reached the restaurant, and the poor man had to take me home. Auntie shared this personal story with strangers. I'm going to kill her.

"The pain takes a long time to go away," Dr. Peleran is saying. "My role is to free up your vertebrae so your own body can repair any damage and return the bones to their correct positions. It's the body's innate intelligence."

My innate intelligence is telling me to run away now. For all I know, the entire town of Fairport knows my intimate secrets.

I take a deep breath, unclench my hands. "May I help you find a book?"

She bustles past me, turns into the Cooking section. "I've only just returned from California. I've *got* to have a cookbook I saw there."

"What book was it?" I can't tell a cookbook from a travel guide, but I pretend to be the next Rachael Ray or Padma Lakshmi or whoever is the current guru of the Food Network.

Lucia touches the books, her red-nailed fingers flitting along the spines like giant lady beetles. "I can't remember the title or the author." A strange look passes across her face—a fleeting expression of terror.

"Can you be more specific?" I gaze at a cryptic ocean of subcategories—diet, diabetic, vegetarian, Chinese, Indian, quick meals, gourmet. Sandwiched in among the new books are collectibles—Betty Crocker, Pillsbury, True Grit. "What letter did the author's name start with? We could look up the book on the computer."

"Computer?" She stares at me blankly, as if all words have tumbled out of her head.

"Are we looking for a type of ethnic cooking?"

She motions with her hands. "Yes, Californian!"

California is not an ethnicity. "What kind of Californian?"

"Wonderful recipes from the coast."

"Okay, a coastal city—Los Angeles, San Francisco."

"No, the East Coast."

"The East Coast of the United States?"

"No, California."

"The east coast of California is Nevada." I keep my voice polite, helpful.

"The book was big, kind of square. There was food on the front—maybe a curry bowl? Maybe a bright green cover. Colorful. Maybe rice? Or noodles. The arrangement was perfect, all the food so appetizing and enticing."

I show her various books, but she keeps shaking her head. The knot tightens in my neck. A high-pitched, quirky voice slides through the air. *It's so beautifully arranged on the plate—you know someone's fingers have been all over it.* The smell of baking muffins drifts in, probably carried on the wind from the bakery down the street.

Lucia goes on talking and talking. A headache creeps across my forehead. I don't care about cookbooks. I don't care about rice or noodles or finding exactly the book she discovered in California. Lucia Peleran and my perfect, happy sister should get together to discuss the menu for the wedding, but I can't stand this another minute.

"Stop!" I say, interrupting her monologue.

She freezes, her mouth half open.

I pull one book off the shelf, then another, and another, and throw them all on the table until they form several tall piles. "Here are cookbooks, dozens of them, hundreds. Just choose one and be done with it!"

Lucia gapes, her mouth opening and closing in slow motion, her eyes blinking. She narrows her gaze at me. "Well," she says, "divorce can make you crazy, too." She snatches a book from the top of a pile, and the whole stack comes crashing down.

Chapter 11

"Another strikeout?" Tony says after Lucia stalks out in a huff.

"I'm not playing baseball here." I shelve the cookbooks, one by one. I don't know what came over me. "We need to get rid of some of the oldest books. Donate them to charity—"

"Don't you dare." Tony grabs *Pasta Galore* from my hands. "Your aunt would have a fit. The old books give this place its character."

"We've got an overload of character here. Way too much stuff."

Tony clutches *Pasta Galore* to his chest, as if the dog-eared paperback holds the key to his survival. "Why do you think your aunt chose you? Not to clean out her inventory!"

"I'm good with numbers. I have a strong business sense. She knows I'll spruce up the store. We need to order in the bestsellers in cooking. We need lights. It's like a cave in here."

"You put this one in the wrong place." Tony pulls a hardcover off the shelf and places it on the next shelf over. "We organize these by subject, then, within the subject, by author."

"Whatever, Tony. Nobody's in here looking, anyway."

"Ruma could have left the store in my hands. I could have done just fine without you. Now you've driven away more than one customer."

"I didn't drive anyone away. Lucia didn't know what she wanted."

Tony points at my forehead. "It's your job to find out."

"I tried."

"Ruma can see things, sense things about people—about what they want and need. She has a kind of third eye."

"That's ridiculous." I make a hocus-pocus motion with my fingers. "Third eye, my ass."

"You can't do this job using only logic. It's not like giving someone a quote on a retirement portfolio."

"They want a book, you give it to them. You figure out what they want."

"Sometimes people don't know what they want. Patience, grace, heart. Compassion. You need those qualities for this job."

"What you need are wider aisles and plush armchairs."

"The armchairs are fine." Tony tucks the pasta book under his arm. "Did you stop to wonder why Lucia flew to California? Not for pleasure, or she would have remembered the name of the cookbook. But she was preoccupied. Her mother owned a house there but could no longer manage the property. She's got some kind of dementia. You could have asked."

"I'm not a psychic, or a psychotherapist."

"Nobody says you have to be." Tony follows me into the Classics section.

"Look, I'm sorry about Lucia's mom. That's sad. But I'm not here to learn her deepest secrets."

"You don't have to. You just have to care. Books are more than commodities to sell. Books hold our culture, our past, other worlds, the antidote for sadness."

"If that were the case, everyone would be flocking to bookstores."

"And maybe they should."

"I've done great without books . . . for years. I don't have time to read anymore."

"Maybe you should make time."

"I've been busy—"

"So you've lost someone, too. I see it in your face. That's all you need. Tap into your humanity. All you need is a little empathy."

"I have empathy." What does he see in my face? There's nothing in my face.

He presses a tattered paperback copy of *Pride and Prejudice* into my hands. "Use your empathy at the Wednesday night reading group. Ruma always leads at the meeting."

"But I don't know how to lead a reading group."

"They usually meet in the tea room."

"But—"

"Do you want to disappoint your aunt?"

"I'm not reading this." I put the book on the table.

He sighs. "Suit yourself. Tomorrow morning Gertrude Gertler is coming in to sign *Fuzzy-Paw Pajamas*."

"*Fuzzy-Paw* . . . ?"

"Gertrude's a little eccentric." He shows me a flat hardcover picture book painted in benign pastels. Fuzzy bears in pajamas.

"What do you mean, 'eccentric'?"

"Oh, you know." He leads me into the parlor. "Just make sure the place is neat, and she can sit there, at that table. Blue Sharpie pen. Pink Post-it Notes."

"Pink Post-it Notes?"

"Write the name of each person who wants a book signed, on the Post-it Note, and hand it to Gertrude so she doesn't misspell the name."

"Do we have pink?"

Tony glances at his watch. "We don't have pink, and Office Onestop is closed. Blue will have to do."

"You'll be here tomorrow to take care of things?"

"I'll make it as soon as I can. I have to ride the ferry, remember?"

I help him arrange the parlor for the book signing, propping a few copies of *Fuzzy-Paw Pajamas* on table displays, along with a selection of Gertrude Gertler's other titles.

"Do we have more books?" I ask. "I count only six copies of *Fuzzy-Paw* and they're all on display."

"Your aunt was in a rush, so the books were ordered at

the last minute, and they're late. But they'll be delivered by courier first thing in the morning."

"First thing. You're sure."

"I'm almost a hundred percent sure." Tony grabs his coat from the closet. On his way out the door, he pauses, his hand on the knob. "You're staying here tonight, right?"

I'm putting on my coat, too. "Why?"

"You told your aunt you would."

"What difference does it make?"

He hesitates, shakes his head. "You can't leave this place alone at night."

"Well, the poor old house will have to brave a few nights alone. It's old enough to take care of itself."

Tony laughs. "Do what you want." And without further explanation, he is gone.

Chapter 12

When I arrive at my parents' house, Gita has gone back to Seattle, and Ma is flitting around in a blue silk sari and a cloud of Joy perfume. She has transformed herself from American to Bengali in one change of clothes and a line of black *kajal* rimming her eyes.

"How was work?" She glances in the hall mirror, turns her head this way and that, jewelry flashing, and pats her short hair.

"Fabulous," I lie, yawning. I drop my handbag in the foyer. "Auntie thinks I'm staying over at the shop. She says the house gets cranky if I don't."

"The house won't know the difference." Ma gives me a bright smile, lit by her twinkling silver earrings. "The Mauliks heard you were in town, and they've invited us all to dinner this evening."

"On such short notice." My heart sinks. She won't let me escape from this one—the Mauliks are old family friends who retired on the island at my parents' urging. Benoy Maulik, my de facto uncle, went to university in India with my father.

"You don't need to dress up," Ma says, patting her hair. "Just go like that."

I glance down at my jeans and sneakers. She can't be serious. Even Dad is dressed up in a silk shirt and slacks and spicy cologne. "I can't go like this. I need to change." Wait—did I just agree to go? I suppose I did.

"Hurry up, then. We need to leave in ten minutes."

Ten minutes! "Why didn't you give me some warning? I'm tired. I think I'll stay home."

Ma pushes me toward the stairs. "What will I tell the Mauliks? After all this time? They're expecting you."

Ten minutes later, I'm ready to go in a paisley blouse and skirt. I'm a kid again, sitting in the backseat of my parents' car as we head to a party at the house of Indian friends. Our parents always left Gita and me in the children's TV room with all the snotty-nosed brats. Gita didn't seem to mind. Five years my junior, she had fun playing with the little ones.

"Has Charu's hip healed?" Ma asks Dad in the front seat. She speaks of Uncle Benoy's wife.

"She's back at work, apparently. Translating Hindi texts for the university."

"Is she still trying to write a novel?"

"She's been writing that book for years," Dad says and laughs.

"Benoy did better after his bypass surgery," Ma says.

"He's looking haggard," Dad says.

"They both look haggard," Ma says.

"He's trying to do too much—always working on some kind of house project—"

"Why doesn't he relax?" Ma says, checking her eyeliner in the overhead mirror. "He'll end up having another heart attack."

My parents' gossip clogs the air like toxic smoke. I roll down the window and inhale the fresh scents of cedar and pine. Years have passed since I sat in the backseat, listening to Ma and Dad discuss other people who aren't present to defend themselves. Do my parents talk about me this way when I'm not around? *That Jasmine, screwed up her marriage. She'll grow old and gray and she'll still be without a husband.*

"The Mauliks have been through a lot, it sounds like," I say, to balance the caustic comments with a dose of charity. "Give them a break."

My parents say nothing as Dad turns onto a manicured, upscale side street and pulls over to the curb. Several cars are parked in front of the Mauliks' house, a two-story stucco box surrounded by lush rhododendrons and fir trees.

I barely recognize the woman who answers the door. Her face is puffy, her black hair limp, her eyes glazed. Auntie Charu, dusky skinned and beautiful, has lost her luster. "Jasmine! So good to see you."

I hug her tightly. "It's been a long time."

"Come in, come in." She steps aside, hugs and kisses my

parents. Inside, the Mauliks' house exudes the essence of India. Kashmiri carpets cover the hardwood floors; statues of Hindu gods perch on teak side tables. In the dining room, silk wall hangings depict scenes from Hindu epics, and in the vast living room, which overlooks the water, an imported couch sits beneath a painting of a battle scene from the Mahabharata. The air carries the odors of wood smoke and heavy spices. The Mauliks have always preserved the memory of their homeland, with such intensity that their homesickness for Bengal seems to ooze from every surface.

My parents' house, on the other hand, mixes artifacts in a blend of East and West, perhaps a result of my father's love of travel and change. He, Ma, and Auntie Ruma were the first in our extended family to emigrate from India. They forged a new path, embracing America with exuberance.

Ma and Dad introduce me to several guests whom I only vaguely recognize. We all gather on the patio and nobody mentions my divorce or my lack of children. The house crawls with the offspring of Indian family friends. Children, especially boys, are the badges of success, and every friend or cousin my age has become a physician, an attorney, a professor.

My father tends the salmon on the barbecue. Uncle Benoy is pouring drinks. My mother is talking to an old friend from India—I recognize her face, but her name eludes me.

I stand awkwardly next to the stone garden wall, pretending to be interested in the rhododendron plants.

"So, Jasmine. You're doing well in business now, nah?"

Uncle Benoy shuffles over to give me a big hug. Since the last time I saw him, a decade ago, his hair has gone completely white.

"I'm doing all right," I say, another lie. The fragility of my position at the firm hits me full force. "You look well, Uncle." His face is lined and gaunt.

"How about that Gita, getting married, nah?"

"We're all looking forward to it," I say politely.

"Drink? Snack for you?" He pats my back.

"Water would be great."

"Water, coming right up." He saunters off.

"Jasmine, is that you?" A long-haired young woman sidles up to me, a cherubic baby girl on her hip.

"Sanchita?" I peer at her. She resembles an elongated version of her childhood self—same dark, oval face and bug eyes—with an added layer of downy black hair on her upper lip. Last time I saw her, she was barely eighteen, three years younger than me. Soon after that, she left for college.

A little boy runs up to her. He's maybe three or four. He's waving a big picture book, *Fuzzy-Paw Pajamas!* "Mom, can you read me this?"

Mom? Sanchita, an only child who received everything her heart desired, has given birth to two children of her own. I'm flabbergasted, and I am feeling older by the minute.

"After supper," she says.

"Ma-a-a."

"Go and play."

He wanders off, pouting.

"Vishnu!" she calls. "Wash your hands before supper."

He nods, not looking back.

"He's cute," I say. My stomach twists. Okay, I'm envious. I don't want her life, but I'm envious of her happy little family, her ability to fulfill everyone else's expectations, her obvious comfort in the role she is supposed to play.

"She's the difficult one," Sanchita says, nodding toward the baby on her hip. The little girl's lips tremble. Her cheeks hang down past her chin. She's beyond cute. She's freshness and new life.

I touch the baby's hot cheeks. "She's adorable, absolutely precious."

"When she wants to be." Sanchita bounces the baby. In pale twilight, the gauntness of Sanchita's face comes into focus, a touch of emptiness in her eyes, as if a part of her has vacated the premises.

"So, I haven't spoken to you in a while. You went away to university. What are you doing now?"

"I'm a physician. Pediatrician."

The word—*pediatrician*—shimmers on her like silk. She is doing what my parents wanted me to do. What her parents wanted her to do. What every Indian parent would want a child to do. She is the quintessential product of an upper-class Bengali family. She has chosen a highly esteemed profession, and she has given birth to a son and the token chubby girl whose cheeks are available for frequent pinching. Nobody could ask for more.

"Congratulations," I say, my throat dry. "Must be a rewarding profession." I bet she lives in a mansion and hires a nanny to care for the kids, unless her husband is a stay-at-home dad.

"Yes, usually pretty rewarding." She's looking over my shoulder at someone behind me. Perhaps I'm not important enough to merit her complete attention. "What about you?"

"I live in L.A. I manage money—retirement portfolios."

She nods, only one-quarter interested. Her baby girl is playing with her hair.

Uncle Benoy returns with my glass of ice water and pinches the baby's cheeks. "How is my little Durga today?" He coos to her in Bengali, which I don't understand, lifts her out of Sanchita's arms, and carries her away to show off to other guests.

Sanchita must expect great things from her children, having named them after powerful deities in the Hindu pantheon.

"And your husband?" I ask. "What does he do?"

"He's a brain surgeon," she says, watching Uncle Benoy walk away with Durga.

My eyebrows rise. What else would he be? "Is he here today? Or is he working? On call? Surgeons work long hours, don't they?"

"Oh, he's here. Family is so important to him."

"That's wonderful." Family was important to Robert, too. He would have started several families with several women, if given half a chance. Lauren won't last long. She's only the latest in Robert's series of fascinations.

"And you? You're married?" Sanchita asks, then licks her

lips. "No, you're separated. Divorced." Someone in her family must have mentioned my plight. *Did you hear about poor Jasmine?*

"Nearly a year ago," I say, keeping a careful smile on my face.

"That's right. He was Indian, or American?"

Was, as if he's now dead. "American." I expect her to say, *Well, that figures.*

"How did you meet him?" she asks.

"Mutual friend, faculty party. He's a professor of anthropology."

She nods. "Wasn't that your major, too?"

"At first, but I switched to something more practical."

"And Gita? She's getting married next spring? To an Indian?"

"So I hear," I say.

A tall, dashing man strides up to us in an open-necked silk shirt and slacks. He could have stepped out of a Bollywood movie, the hero of an epic tale. He is comfortable, in command of his space. If I had married a man like him, would my life be different?

"Darling," he says to Sanchita in a smooth voice, touched by a slight Bengali accent. His eyes fill with adoration for her. "Your mother would like help in the kitchen."

"Tell her I'm coming," Sanchita says.

He turns to me and smiles. Perfect white teeth. "I'm Sanchita's husband, Mohan, and you are . . . ?"

"Jasmine. Nobody's wife." I'm not a mother, and I'm a sorry excuse for a bookseller. I can manage stock portfolios like nobody's business, but I'm almost out of a job.

Sanchita and Mohan look at me blankly.

"Never mind," I say. "A lame joke."

"Sanchita!" Auntie Charu calls.

"Ma, I'm coming!" Sanchita shouts back. Her voice regresses to childhood as she and Mohan rush off.

We all stay on the patio for supper, and the evening blurs into animated conversations about politics and religion, travel and physics, astronomy and literature. I start to enjoy the banter, the company of family friends, and the food—spicy salmon, basmati rice, savory *dal*, and sweet desserts.

For a time, the weight of expectations falls away. The wine helps, dulling my pain, soothing the sharpness of sad memories. My mind grows fuzzy, and later, back at my parents' house, I have no trouble sleeping, for the first time in nearly a year.

But in the morning, when I return to the bookstore, Tony is bustling around, cursing under his breath. "You didn't stay over, did you? I came in early. I had a bad feeling. Now look what we have to deal with."

I look around, my mouth dropping open. "What the hell happened here?"

Chapter 13

The parlor is a mess—books pulled off shelves, furniture moved. Gertrude's picture books are on the floor, the display replaced by a series of classics by Beatrix Potter, E. B. White, Lewis Carroll, and other dead authors.

I head for the door, my heart pounding. "I'll call the police."

"No, don't." Tony rushes up and blocks my way. "Nothing was stolen. I checked the till."

"But the place has been vandalized."

"Not vandalized. Rearranged." He picks up a copy of *Shakespeare's Sonnets*.

"What do you mean, 'rearranged'?"

"Happens sometimes. Everything's here; it's just not where it's supposed to be."

"How do you know? Have you accounted for all the books?"

"Pretty much. This is the only room affected."

"My aunt needs an alarm system. . . ."

"We don't need an alarm system here. This is not L.A." Tony pushes an armchair away from the wall.

"Obviously you do need one. Someone has broken in!"

"Nobody broke in."

A ripple of ice travels through my body. "Are you saying that someone was already inside?"

"Yeah, maybe."

"Then where is he now? Why would anyone do this?"

"Maybe someone doesn't want us focusing on Gertrude."

I shelve *The Wind in the Willows*. "Right. These dead authors would rather we focus on their books instead?"

"Maybe. Ask them."

I laugh. "Come on, Tony. Did you do this?"

His glare could cut through stone. "Why would I make a mess, only to have to clean it up? How does that make any sense? What would be my motivation?"

I pick up a giant volume from the floor, an old hardcover copy of *Alice in Wonderland*. "To punish me for not staying overnight? I don't know. To scare me? Maybe you want me to live here twenty-four/seven, so you can take some time off."

"Believe me, I'm not going to abandon Ruma's store now." He snatches the book from my hand. "I told you to stay. You could've prevented all this. It had nothing to do with me."

"You can't actually believe the house is cranky. You believe in my aunt's whims?"

"I wouldn't call them whims." He purses his lips. "And your aunt is no dummy."

"Do you really believe . . . ?"

"What I believe doesn't matter." He glances at his watch. "We have to get this room tidy. We need to set the coffee and tea brewing. Gertrude will arrive soon. I'm not looking forward to dealing with this mess every day while you're here."

"Every day? This is going to happen every day?"

"Maybe worse. We'll have to rearrange all the furniture. Biographies and memoirs could end up in Mystery. Mystery in Romance. Romance in Reference—"

"So this has happened before?"

He frowns, hesitating, then says, "Your aunt told me she used to go away now and then, but every time she left, something would be out of place when she returned. One small thing. An antique pen moved from the parlor to the office. Tea leaves scattered on the countertop. It got worse over time. Last year she took a weekend trip to Portland, for a trade show, and the store was a mess when she got back. Took her two days to clean up. She hardly ever goes away now. This trip to India is huge for her."

As if in protest, a dusty paperback slips off the shelf, followed by a cascade of falling books.

"She could have warned me," I say.

"Would you still have come?" He puts the book away and straightens the shelves.

"I probably wouldn't have believed her."

"There you go."

"Why don't you stay over, Tony, and keep the store company?"

"It can't be just anyone," he says.

This is ridiculous. On the wall, a faded photograph of

Lewis Carroll hangs askew. I straighten the picture, labeled *Charles Lutwidge Dodgson*, Lewis Carroll's real name. In a dark jacket, high-collared white shirt, and bow tie, he's sitting in profile, revealing his left side, right hand raised to his cheek. Long-faced, sad. "Did you do this?" I ask him.

Mr. Dodgson turns toward me. I step back, losing my breath. No, he's still looking to the side, his pensive gaze cast downward.

"You okay?" Tony says.

I'm suffering from mild hallucinations. Maybe I had too much wine last night. "I need coffee," I say quickly. "I need to clear my mind."

A whole shelf of hardcovers tips over like a series of dominoes.

"The house is annoyed," Tony says, shaking his head.

I hold up my hands. "You win. I'll stay here tonight, if that's what I have to do."

Silence descends. I make for the door. The prospect of a night here makes my chest constrict. These vast rooms won't keep me company. Nobody will sleep beside me. Robert will slip into bed next to Lauren, pull her into his arms. And I will be lost in an ancient, crumbling Victorian mansion in the middle of nowhere.

As I approach the door, a matte poster of William Shakespeare brightens in a shaft of sunlight—a reproduction of a realistic color portrait. His forehead shines, a silver earring glinting in his left ear. His lips turn up at the corners. *O that infected moisture of his eye, / O that false fire which in his cheek so glow'd.*

"I'm impressed. You know your Shakespeare." I turn to Tony, but he's on the other side of the room, facing away from me, whistling a soft, tuneless melody.

Chapter 14

Outside, a small group of parents and toddlers gathers on the sidewalk. They're bundled up, chatting and hopping around in the cold, their breath rising into puffs of steam. So this is the extent of our book-signing crowd for Gertrude Gertler.

"We don't have enough books," Tony says. "I may need to go to Seattle—"

"There are maybe seven people outside. Not exactly a crowd."

"I need to call the courier. Best-case scenario, the books are still on their way."

"My aunt should have advertised the event, put up flyers, sent announcements to the schools—"

"She's been preoccupied."

I feel stricken at this reminder of my aunt's illness. "She still needs a business to come back to."

"She's done okay up until now." Tony pivots and heads for the office. I follow, close on his heels.

"She can't be doing okay. We need a monthly calendar, flyers, a plan of action. That will be your job, to make up flyers. My aunt put me in charge, and I'm giving you the task of advertising her events."

"Whatever you say," Tony says, flinging open the office door. "You're the boss. You know everything about this store, obviously. You're so . . . perceptive."

"Is that irony? Are you mocking me? I couldn't know the parlor would be messed up, for whatever reason."

He rolls his eyes. "You waltz in here and think you can fix this place. But first you need to open your eyes, see what's right in front of you."

I look around, at the piles of dusty books, the dim corners, cobwebs hanging from the ceiling. I had already wiped down those windowsills, but they are dusty again. "I see what's in front of me, and it's not a pretty sight."

Tony shakes his head, as if I am incorrigible. "We need to focus on Gertrude. I'm calling the courier." He disappears into the office, slamming the door in my face.

There's a tentative knock on the front door, the one facing the waterfront, away from the customers. I open the door to find a diminutive woman, bundled in layers of knitted winter clothing, standing huddled on the porch, her pink nose planted like a cherry in the middle of a round face.

"We're not open yet," I say. "Can you wait around the corner with the others?"

She pushes past me into the house and unwinds the knitted scarf from around her neck. "What took you so long?" she says in a raspy voice. "I almost caught my death of cold out there." She folds the scarf into a neat square and places it on a table.

"If you could wait outside—"

"Don't you know who I am?" She pulls off the knitted cap, and a sparse collection of downy silver hairs stands straight upward in a glorious blaze of static electricity. She folds the cap and puts it on the table next to her scarf.

"You're . . . Gertrude Gertler?" My cheeks heat up. "I didn't recognize you in your winter clothes." And whoever took her author photos performed wondrous feats of visual magic.

"I don't know how anyone could *not* recognize me." She pulls off her mittens and folds and places them on the table, too. "Where is my tea?"

"We've had a bit of trouble here this morning, so we've fallen behind."

"What kind of trouble?" She rubs the palms of her tiny hands together. "You don't have tea? I always have tea when I come here."

I usher her into the tea room and set the kettle on the stove. "Can I get you a glass of water, apple juice, orange juice?"

"I always have tea." She's still rubbing her hands together. "I don't drink juice. Didn't Ruma tell you?"

"Of course, tea." She's a diva.

"Let me see where I'll be signing."

"In the parlor. But the room is still a mess." I lead her down the hall. When she steps into the parlor, she trembles like a volcano about to erupt.

"Where. Are. My. Books?" she says.

Tony rushes in to fix the displays. "We have six for now. We'll have more later."

"You. Have. Six?" She throws up her hands and lets out a wail. "Only six? Did you see all those people out there?"

All what people? A few of them seem to have wandered off. I count four adults and two toddlers on the sidewalk.

"We'll work it out," Tony says. "The courier was delayed in Portland."

"Oregon! He'll take hours to get here." She strides to the signing table, picks up the packet of blue Post-it Notes. "What are these?"

"They're for you," Tony says. "We'll do the usual—write down the names so you can sign the books and spell everything correctly."

"But they're blue." Her voice trembles on a high wire.

Tony glances over her head at me. I shrug and shake my head. "I'm so sorry," he says. "We don't have pink Post-it Notes today."

She throws the blue pack on the table. "I made it perfectly clear. I spelled it out. I require pink Post-it Notes. I can't see the writing on blue. And where is my blue Sharpie pen?"

"We'll find one for you." Tony motions to me to look for a pen.

I turn and head back to the office. The kettle is whistling, and someone is knocking on the door. I run to turn off the stove, pour a pot of English breakfast tea, and rush back to the office. I rummage through Auntie's supplies, but I can't find a single blue Sharpie marker. They're all black. What is wrong with this Gertrude woman?

I take her a cup of tea and a black pen. "I hope this will work."

She shakes her head and tosses the pen on the table. She ignores the cup of tea. "My requirements are minimal. Pink notes, blue pen, a neat and tidy room, and my *books*. And a cup of tea when I walk in the door. I came a long way for this event." She's heading back to the tea room, where she gathers her scarf and hat and mittens off the table. She's making for the door.

Tony tugs my sleeve. "Got any ideas for fixing this one? We need an idea right now. She came in looking for investment books once. . . . Give her some free advice?"

"You want me to grovel at the feet of a snotty author just so she'll stay to sign a couple of her books?"

"Why not? The kids love her." Tony's staring out the window at the small crowd on the sidewalk. I follow his gaze. Gertrude is bundled up again, hurrying away to her car. Maybe I should go after her. She glances back over her shoulder and frowns in our direction. No, let her go.

Chapter 15

An hour later, fifty-seven copies of *Fuzzy-Paw Pajamas* are piled on the parlor table.

"We have to get Gertrude back in," Tony says.

"Can't we send back the books?"

"But the kids love her. Did you see their faces when you told them Gertrude had canceled? They were devastated."

I feel a twinge beneath my ribs. "There are worse things in life than missing a book signing. They'll get over it."

"You're such a Scrooge. You're nothing like your aunt."

I clench my jaw and focus on cleaning up the room. How does my aunt fit so many books into one small space? "Nobody said I was like her."

"Weren't you ever a kid?"

"Nope." I shelve a copy of *Inner Peace for Busy People*. How did this book end up on the floor?

"Gertrude makes the kids laugh. Do you ever laugh?"

I swallow a dry lump in my throat. "Laughter is overrated."

"Don't you ever have fun?"

"Actually, I'm going on a date Friday night. If you call that fun." I had nearly forgotten. Had Connor even been real? What will he expect from me? I'll be alone with him here.

Tony's eyebrows rise, his whole forehead lifting beneath his slicked-back bangs. "You?"

"Don't look so surprised. His name is Connor Hunt. He's a doctor, just visiting. I don't even know how to reach him, so I can't cancel."

"A doctor! Why would you want to cancel?"

"Because I don't date. But I agreed to it this time . . . Never mind. It was almost like a voice told me to go out with him and I stupidly listened."

Tony drops a book on his foot and winces. "You what? You heard a voice?"

"Not really. Maybe it was the wind."

Tony picks up the book. "Come here and sit down." He directs me to an armchair next to a pivoting lamp. Then he shines the light in my face.

I shield my eyes. "Turn that thing the other way."

"I'm checking for your third eye."

"I am not my aunt. She believes in that kind of garbage. I do not."

But Tony's eyes are wide, and he's shaking his head. "Girl, you have it. You have the third eye. You probably did hear voices. Your aunt hears them, too."

I push him away and get up. "Your voice is the only one I'm hearing, and if you saw anything on my forehead, it was probably a zit."

"Excuse me?" A young owl-eyed woman pops her head in the door. Her features are round and fixed, as if she must also turn her head the way an owl does, all at once, without moving the eyes. "Does anyone work in this place?"

"She does," Tony says, pointing at me. "She has the third eye."

"Tony." I give him a warning look, then smile at the woman. "How can I help you?" I follow her into the hall.

She gives me a suspicious look. "Do you have diuretics?"

"Diuretics," I say, blinking. I don't usually need them. "I don't think my aunt carries them. Maybe try the pharmacy?"

"No, diuretics. It's more a science than a religion."

"Dianetics," Tony says.

She breaks out in a big smile. "That's it exactly."

I blink. "But you said—"

Tony steers the woman toward a shelf. "Sometimes people don't know exactly what they mean. You have to interpret."

The owl-eyed woman nods enthusiastically. She leaves with two books about Dianetics. How was I to know?

Near closing time, a stooped, wild-haired man slips into the parlor and begins straightening books in an obsessive-compulsive way. When he sees me, his bushy brows twitch. "Who are you?" His eyes flit from side to side.

"I'm Jasmine. I'll be here for a few weeks." I look around, but Tony is nowhere in sight.

The man pulls a wrinkled white handkerchief from his pocket and wipes his forehead. "Harold Avery. Professor to you." He tucks the handkerchief back into his pocket. Then his fingers are moving, touching the books, straightening them again. "I'm going to, let me see . . . India. Which travel guide is best, in your experience?"

I want to tell him I haven't been to India in years, but I'm already heading toward the Travel section. A golden book glows in a shaft of slanted afternoon sunlight. Written across the spine in red letters are the words *Magic in the Mango Orchards*. The scent of mangoes rises into my nose. Must be the man's unusual cologne.

I choose the newest Fodor's guide to India.

The professor frowns. "Boring."

"Fodor's is reliable," I say.

"I don't want reliable. I want different." Fodor's ends up on the shelf. His fingers run along the tops of the books again, like tiny pattering cockroaches.

I keep handing him travel books, one after another, but nothing is good enough.

"Jasmine—is any book jumping out at you?" Tony is standing in the doorway. "Or glowing? Or sticking out? The right books always stick out for Ruma."

Professor Avery nods, as if this is a common occurrence in most bookstores.

"Not exactly." I almost laugh at the absurdity. "What do you mean, 'sticking out'?"

A deep voice speaks nearby. *"The first condition of understanding a foreign country is to smell it."*

"Who said that?" I say, glancing around. "Tony?"

"Said what?" Tony says.

Professor Avery keeps touching the books.

I look at him suspiciously. "Something about understanding a foreign country by its smell. Like the scent of mango or something—"

"Wasn't me," the professor says.

"Rudyard Kipling," Tony says, staring at me.

T.S. Eliot misquoted me, the same deep voice says. Kipling? Can't be. Tony and the professor are grinning at me, as if they know something I don't know. I edge away from the mysterious voice, toward the door, ready for a quick escape.

Chapter 16

After the professor leaves empty-handed, Tony pats my shoulder. "You're hearing the dead speak. Congratulations."

"I don't know what game you're playing," I say, "but it won't work with me." Outside, a fir branch scrapes the window, its high-pitched screech like a distant voice.

"Kipling spoke to you. Don't deny it." Tony snatches a book from the shelf and waves it, a vintage hardcover copy of *The Jungle Book*, in front of my face.

I pull back. "What are you doing? Get that thing out of my face."

"Does this conjure any other images? Maybe Kipling's broom mustache, bushy brows, receding hairline? Pointy ears?"

I push the book away. "I have no idea what Kipling was like in person."

"But he did speak to you." Tony follows me as I leave the

room. Sunlight dances in colors on the hallway wall, filtered through the stained-glass window. He's still brandishing the book. "Woo-woo, Jasmine, the ghosts are talking."

"No, you are talking. Do you play these tricks on Auntie Ruma? Must drive her crazy." I grab my cell phone from the back pocket of my jeans, out of habit. No signal, as usual. But then a face pops onto the screen. Broom mustache, bushy brows, receding hairline, pointy ears. A mischievous grin. *Kipling.*

Impossible. My hands tremble, and I nearly drop the phone. Then the face disappears; the display goes blank. The cell phone vibrates in my hand, and the casing seems to darken until it becomes a mere shadow against the backdrop of my skin. The image must have been a trick of the sunlight, which has followed me in here, settling on a stack of books. The titles glow. *Across the Threshold, Accepting the Call, The Truth as I See It.*

I feel suddenly claustrophobic. "I . . . need some air. I'm taking a break for a few minutes."

"Jasmine, wait—"

"I'll be back." I throw on my coat and run out into the cool, crisp afternoon. A robin lands in the glistening grass and pecks at an invisible worm. The autumn air brushes my face. The remaining poplar leaves, the ones that refuse to fall, rustle gently against one another.

High in the sky, Canadian geese pass overhead, honking their way to somewhere new. I hurry along the brick sidewalk, sloughing off the oppressive disorder of the bookstore. Kipling's image formed the way dreams form, a mere simulacrum of what is real. The island itself, blustery and rocky, wet and mossy, inhospitable and unyielding, is what's real.

Five blocks up, two blocks over, my cell phone registers a faint display in symmetrical green bars. Relief. I'm once again connected to the ordinary world, to what I can predict and understand. I check my voice-mail box, then call back three clients who want updates on their retirement accounts. I'm happy to hear them speak, and yet, I'm already distant from their harried, distracted voices.

My boss, Scott Taylor, left me a message. *We're moving up your presentation to the day after you get back. The client is anxious to get moving on this. I'll be in Seattle next week. I'll come out to see you. We'll discuss strategy. Where the hell are these islands, anyway? Okay, I'm look-ing at the map. Jeez, you're in the middle of nowhere. I'll have to take a boat.*

Next a garbled message comes through from Robert in a haze of static. *Condo . . . talk . . . call . . . left messages. . . .* I hit the Delete button with glee and retrace my steps to the bookstore. The wind has subsided. Seagulls call from the shore, where low tide coughs up secrets and the dank smell of kelp. My shoe slips on a patch of moss, and I nearly fall on the sidewalk. Did Captain Vancouver slide on moss when he first set foot on these islands? The moss is everywhere, insidious, growing from cracks, on walls, in thin layers on rooftops. The moss always felt like part of me when I was a child—like a spongy gateway to alternate worlds.

Now it's a health hazard.

In the foyer of the bookstore, Tony zips up his raincoat, which he turns up at the collar like Sam Spade. "I thought you got eaten by a werewolf. Or maybe a sea monster rose up and snatched you away."

"Stranger things have happened," I say, shivering.

"Yeah, like, book groups meet here. Their members actually buy books. I wish I could stay for tonight's meeting, but I'm late for the ferry. *Pride and Prejudice* awaits you, my dear."

I press the back of my hand to my forehead. "Why does my aunt waste time with book groups? Can't they meet on their own? I need to look into ordering new titles and clean up some more, and I should sift through the bills on her desk—"

"I caught up with that. See you tomorrow."

"Can't you stay?" A headache ripples at the back of my neck.

"Your mom brought your luggage. You're all set. You'll do fine." He slicks back his hair with the flats of his hands. And he is gone. Auntie was right. People are always disappearing around here.

Chapter 17

The first person to arrive for the book group is Lucia Pel-eran, in pastel pants, an oversized sweater that resembles a hot air balloon about to launch, and white running shoes anchoring her to earth.

She takes my hands in her bony claws. "How are you hold-ing up? I know life doesn't seem worthwhile now, but there's hope." She seems to have forgotten the cookbook fiasco.

"I'm doing well, thanks." I extract my hands from her grip. I could pretend I'm going to slit my throat, or fling a rope over the rafters and create a makeshift noose, to see the look on her face.

She lowers her voice, blasts me with her peppermint breath. "I did exactly what you did, sleeping on one side of the bed even though there was a whole king-sized bed to stretch out in. Hard to break the marriage habit, isn't it? I used to curl up in the smallest space, because my ex-husband took up so much room. Men always do. But after a few months, I realized, what the heck? I can sleep diagonally if I want to. I can throw my books on the covers, I can eat dinner and drop crumbs, and I can jump on the mattress."

Auntie told this stranger that *I sleep on one side of the bed?* "Enjoy the jumping. I prefer a good night's sleep," I say. "Can I get you anything? Tea? Coffee?"

"I'll head on back and put the kettle on." She strides right past me, giving me a sharp look.

I follow her into the tea room, my shoulders tense. "I can make the tea."

"No need. Virginia takes hers stronger than usual, to boost her spirits. I know how to make it. Five Earl Grey bags. She's coming tonight, you know. Her boutique isn't doing so well in this economy, but I told her, stop carrying those nine-hundred-dollar silk blouses and you'll do a whole lot better."

"Nine hundred dollars?"

"To serve the high-end clientele from the city." Lucia bustles around in the tea room, putting on the kettle, extracting cups and a tray. Her clothes fade and suddenly she's wearing an apron, her hair curled and sweaty, as she turns to place a tray of muffins on a countertop. Bright oven mitts appear on her hands, like bright red boxing gloves. I blink, and the image dissipates. She's back in her tight pants and balloon sweatshirt, holding only a teacup.

She frowns at me. "Are you okay? You look pale."

"I'm okay, it's just— Do you like baking?"

"Baking? What, baking? Baking what? As if I have time for hobbies."

"You were looking for a cookbook. Maybe about pastries and desserts?"

Her eyes widen, and she nearly drops the teacup. "How did you know?"

Try The Way to Cook, a high-pitched voice says. *One of my best efforts.*

"Excuse me?" I spin around. Tony's not in here. He can't be the one throwing his voice. "One of whose best efforts?"

"What?" Lucia says. "Is that a book?"

"I'm not sure." My mind is muddled. Baking—furious flour and spacious sugar—is her alchemy of healing, for Lucia's pain hides in a deeper place than mine, in a dark well inside her. Why are these images coming to me?

But outwardly, she seems so vibrant, so . . . together. She dispenses lighthearted advice about how I will survive, but somehow I know that she will not survive without baking, without the spirit of Julia Child.

"Let me know if you remember, hon." Lucia sinks into the couch with a mug of tea in hand, crosses one leg over the other, and swings her foot.

A tall woman glides in a moment later, resplendent in a flowing blue and white pantsuit, like the frothy wake behind a speeding boat. She introduces herself as Virginia Langemack, grabs her cup of tea, arranges herself in an armchair across from Lucia, screws up her nose, and looks around the room. She takes in the Tiffany lamps and the rickety bookshelves on which Auntie has placed used books, magazines, and old board games. Several other women arrive in a range of outfits, shapes, and sizes. The room is abuzz with lively conversation.

"Jasmine, give us your bookseller's literary wisdom," Lucia says after she has shushed everyone.

"I have no special knowledge," I say, shaking my head.

"Oh?" Virginia places her cup and saucer on the table in front of her and stirs in a dollop of cream. A heavy silver bracelet glints on her wrist. "Then why on earth would your aunt bother to bring you here?"

I freeze. Lucia clucks her tongue. "Oh, Ginnie, you know this situation is temporary. Ruma's coming back."

"But why her? This Jasmine?"

"Why not?" Lucia says.

A key turns inside me, a subtle unlocking. "I can help my aunt get this shop in order."

"Fine, let's see what you can do." Virginia glares at me.

Lucia pulls out her dog-eared copy of *Pride and Prejudice*. "This book was originally called *First Impressions*. I looked it up."

Virginia slurps her tea. "That's a stupid name for a book." A mysterious breeze ruffles her hair, leaving a couple of strands sticking straight up, as if electrified.

Lucia forges on. "More important, it's about how first impressions can deceive you."

The breeze subsides.

Another woman says, "I've heard that authors think of many titles for their books before they settle on a final one."

Virginia keeps slurping. "Both titles are silly." Her silver bracelet slips off her wrist and falls on the hardwood. "The clasp broke!" She reaches down, fumbles around on the floor. "Where the heck did it go?"

"I'll help you." I get on my hands and knees. The bracelet fell impossibly far from where she is sitting. "Here it is."

"Thank you." When she sits straight again, several new strands of hair are sticking out. I stifle a smile.

Lucia pulls a pocket notebook from her purse, licks her thumb, and flips to the first page. "Was Jane Austen a realist? Charlotte Brontë said her work was like a 'carefully fenced, highly cultivated garden.' Ralph Waldo Emerson said that her depiction of life was 'pinched and narrow.'"

A creaking sound comes from the hallway. We all glance in that direction.

"Mark Twain thought libraries shouldn't carry her books," Lucia goes on. "But I say don't pay any attention to jealous authors. She wrote a masterpiece. I love this book every time I read it—because it makes me believe we can overcome any obstacle."

Every time she reads it?

Virginia tucks her broken bracelet into her purse. "I'm not fond of so much dialogue without any description." Her arm bumps into her cup, tipping it over and spilling tea on the table.

I jump to my feet, grab napkins, and dab at the liquid. "I'll get towels. Carry on."

Lucia laughs. "The house is angry with you, Ginnie."

Everyone turns to me. My heart skips a beat, but I smile.

"So, Jasmine," Virginia says, glaring at me, "you have to give us the key question."

"The key question?" I blink.

"You did read the book, didn't you?" Virginia stares at me.

"Your aunt poses an important question about the book, but if you didn't read it—"

"Of course I read it." A long time ago. I hold up the soggy towels. "I'll go and put these in the wash."

I run to the laundry room, take a few deep breaths. What question, what question? I read this book so long ago.

Their voices drift down the hall.

"Consider Mr. Wickham," a woman says behind me. Her voice is musical, touched by a soft English accent.

I spin around. Did one of the women follow me? Nobody's here.

Complex odors spread through the air—dried horse manure, wood smoke, roses, and sweat. As if someone has entered the room, someone who makes fires, tends a farm—someone who bathes maybe once a week and wears cologne to mask her body odor.

"What do you mean about Mr. Wickham?" I say. Mr. Wickham, the smooth-talking young soldier who tricks Elizabeth Bennet into believing the worst about stoic Mr. Darcy. But Mr. Wickham turns out to be a scoundrel. I knew my own Mr. Wickham, someone I trusted. Someone I wanted to trust.

"You know the story better than you think."

My mind spins. The smells grow in intensity, and fabric swishes—a dress rustling nearby. "I haven't read the book in years," I whisper to the empty room.

"You must learn to trust your instincts."

"Why? . . . Virginia, is that you?" I'm talking to myself in my aunt's laundry room. The perfumed detergent must be poisoning my mind. But what of the horse manure odor? Smoke?

There's a soft sigh. "Virginia is insufferable."

"Stop this," I say. I press my hands to my temples.

The strange smells disappear, and only a faint lemon scent remains. There's an absence in the room, as if someone has left.

I take deep breaths, my head spinning.

I shuffle back to the parlor, holding out my hand to brace myself against the wall as I go. When I step inside, everyone stares at me.

"You look pale," Lucia says. "Will you sit down?"

The women all murmur. "You're not feeling well?" "Is everything okay?"

"I have my question. About the book," I say. My voice sounds distant, as if someone else is speaking. "Consider Mr. Wickham's function in the novel."

"Go on," Lucia says, staring at me.

"Think in terms of the geometry of desire. What is the source of Elizabeth's attraction to Mr. Wickham?" Where am I getting this?

"She believes he's good," a small, round woman says. "He's everything she wants—handsome, accessible. He's not proud. She can talk to him."

That was my ex-husband, Robert. He had me fooled, too. "What role does he play in her attraction to Mr. Darcy? What is the significance of his love affairs?"

There's a silence, then Lucia says, "He represents her preconceived notions—what appears on the surface versus what's underneath. So it really is about first impressions."

"Exactly," I say.

"How did you come up with this question?" Virginia asks, her gaze prickly.

"I have no idea. I didn't even read the book, at least, not recently." The knot tightens in the back of my neck. All eyes are on me. The house creaks; the floorboards groan as they settle. The walls breathe dust. Virginia is shaking her head, skeptical. What does she think, that I ran off to read the CliffsNotes on *Pride and Prejudice*?

"I knew it." Lucia slaps the table. "I knew Jasmine would know just what to say."

Toxic black mold must be growing here, making me hear things, smell things. I'm allergic to laundry detergent, or maybe a tumor is growing on my brain. The house will have to throw another tantrum tonight. I'm not staying past dark.

After I bid the book group good-bye, I run up to the apartment to grab my luggage. My suitcase thumps all the way down the stairs.

The wind picks up, blasting the house, and to the west, twilight drops a gray blanket across the sky. As I reach to open the heavy front door, a shadow falls across the foyer, and a familiar baritone voice slides across my skin. "Jasmine, wait. You're leaving us so soon?"

Chapter 18

"Connor, you scared me half to death." My suitcase tips over, the handle slipping from my fingers. I hastily yank it upright again. "What are you doing here?"

"I was hoping to catch you. Looks like you're going away." He steps in front of me, blocking my path to the door. He has just arrived from somewhere, the smell of the outside air and a hint of wood smoke still clinging to his clothes. He has a fondness for travel jackets, cargo pants, and hiking boots.

"I'm closing up the store." I dangle the bookstore keys in the air between us. "I'm staying with my parents down the road."

"You're open until eight, another half hour."

"I know, but I have to close early. Will you come back tomorrow? I'm in a hurry." I try to brush past him, but my suitcase has gained a couple hundred pounds.

"You'll return in the morning?" he says, sounding worried. A faint halo surrounds him, the glow from a Tiffany lamp.

"Before the store opens." My suitcase wheels are turning now, but the front door seems to be welded shut.

"I'll try to stop in before work," he says. He opens the front door with ease and steps out onto the porch. How did he manage that? His dark hair shines in the pale porch light.

I drag my suitcase out after him and turn to lock the deadbolts from the outside. "Still can't get the hang of this." I jiggle one key this way and that. Three ancient deadbolts, three different keys. Finally I succeed, but when I turn around, Connor is gone. He's nowhere on the porch, the sidewalk, or the street. He has disappeared again, but my cell phone is beeping.

"Wow, a signal! That's strange." I flip open the phone.

"Finally," my best friend, Carol, says. "Where have you been? I've been trying to reach you for two days."

"I'm in the remote wilderness," I say to her distant, crackling voice. "I could lose you at any second. I don't usually get a signal here at the bookstore."

"Hope you'll be flying back here on time. Bill Youngman wants the Hoffman account. He's been pestering Scott for it, trying to hint that you're unreliable."

I squeeze my phone so tight, the metal might buckle. "He's lying. I'm totally reliable."

"I know that, and you know that, and Scott won't give in, yet. You need to make your usual perfect presentation. Are you preparing?"

"I'll practice tonight. I'm thinking of flying back early, on standby."

"Having that much fun, huh?" I hear her children yelling in the background. "Gotta go. Oh, wait. I meant to tell you. Don and I got a sitter last night. We went to Andante. You know, first Tuesday and all."

"And?" My skin prickles. Andante, a romantic Italian waterfront restaurant where Carol and her husband and Robert and I used to go for dinner the first Tuesday night of each month, a tradition. I'd forgotten—or blocked out the memory.

"You wouldn't believe it. Robert was there with that woman."

The keys fall on the porch with a hollow thud. I bend to pick them up. My fingers are trembling. I drop the keys into my coat pocket. "This isn't something I want to know."

"She was wearing this strapless black thing. She might as well have been naked. The slut."

The phone shakes in my hand. "Carol, I—"

"I wasn't going to tell you, but Don said I should. He went up to talk to them. Of course I had to go with him or I would've looked rude."

"Of course," I say. My lips are going numb. My teeth are chattering. Robert is still destroying me from a distance.

"They were holding hands across the table, just like you and Robert used to do. I felt like telling him, this is *our* restaurant. He shouldn't have brought her there."

I'm silent, stunned, the words gone from my mind.

"Jasmine? Look, I'm sorry for telling you. Robert asked about you—he said he needed to talk to you. He was trying to reach you. I said you were on a wild, fantastic vacation on a beautiful island in the middle of nowhere and for all I knew, you could have fallen in love again."

My heart is racing. "Thanks, Carol. You didn't tell him where I was?"

"He kept asking me for details, like it was still any of his business. The slut was not happy. She started fidgeting, and she wasn't smiling anymore. I didn't tell him a thing, but he had that jealous look. The nerve of him, after he cheated on you and there he was sitting there with *her*. He wanted to have his cake and eat it, too. Maybe you shouldn't come back. Let the guy wonder where you are, and serves him right."

I lose the signal, and Carol's voice vanishes into the night. "Serves him right," I echo. My fragile heart, which had begun to heal, shatters into fine fragments.

Suddenly I'm not so eager to leave Auntie's bookstore. Why not stay here, where Robert can't reach me, no matter how hard he tries? I turn off my phone, unlock the door, and step back into the darkness.

Chapter 19

I can't believe I'm here, lying in Auntie's sagging bed in her attic apartment as a midnight windstorm wails across the island. The house groans and shudders. Rain pummels the roof, the roar of its wrath as loud as an airplane engine. A triangular window, set high on the wall beneath the peaked ceiling, trembles and shakes, threatening to break. The bedside lamp, stained glass imprinted with monarch butterflies, flickers.

I sink back into the pillows. No TV, no cell phone signal. Nothing but books piled on the bedside table, including a collection of Edgar Allan Poe short stories. Bad idea to read about the horrors of reanimated dead bodies while I'm trying to survive in a haunted mansion.

I can't dispel the image of Robert in Andante with Lauren. What did I do to deserve his unfaithfulness? Was it already hardwired into him? He said he fell in love accidentally. I knew her only in passing, as one of Robert's colleagues at the university. I detected no trace of deception, and yet . . . was she already sleeping with him when I met her at a faculty dinner?

I get up, insomniac that I am, and peruse Auntie's shelves in her tiny living room. A draft whooshes in through an open window, ruffling the pages of a book perched on the sill. *The House at Pooh Corner.* Scrawled inside the front cover are the words in black ink,

Jasmine, don't be afraid to start again. . . . A. A. Milne

The handwriting leans backward, and a couple of small ink blotches mar the page. Auntie must have written this. A. A. Milne could not have penned the words. He died years ago and left only his books, his characters, his imagination.

Auntie is playing an elaborate joke. She remembered that Winnie the Pooh was one of my favorite characters, many years ago. No, Eeyore was. He had such trouble spelling; he signed his own name as *eoR*. In which book did he write *rissolution* on a document for Christopher Robin?

I make chamomile tea and put on my reading glasses. I flop into bed and open the book, which emits a newly minted smell. I flip through, hold the pages to my nose, and inhale. I'm a child again, opening brand-new books from Auntie. *Winnie the Pooh, The Chronicles of Narnia*, and Dr. Seuss: *The Cat in the Hat, Green Eggs and Ham*. A long time ago, I read the stories over and over. I had no cares in the world. My heart had not yet been broken.

> *One day when Pooh Bear had nothing else to do, he thought*
> *he would do something, so he went round to Piglet's house*
> *to see what Piglet was doing. . . .*

The lights promptly wink off.

"Great!" I drop the book on the bed. The night-light plugged into the wall still glows, perhaps from battery power. The walls vibrate, and a broom clatters to the floor. I nearly jump out of my nightgown. My heart pounds.

"Okay, you're okay," I tell myself. "It's just an outage in a windstorm."

What am I even doing here?

Defying Robert, that's what.

I grab the flashlight from the bureau and tiptoe down the dusty servants' staircase.

In the second-floor hallway, a fan of white wallpaper has peeled back to reveal an ancient floral pattern underneath. The rose petal imprint shines in metallic red and blue.

"Fuse box, first floor." I tiptoe down the hall to the wide main staircase, which runs up to the second floor from the first-floor entry hall, facing the waterfront. I'm on the second step down when I hear faint voices. I stop cold, my legs rubbery. Must be the wind in the trees.

The flashlight beam plays across the colored glass. Just a few more steps down, back through the hall, past the parlor, library, and dining room. I can do it. As I approach the bottom step, the voices rise again. No, it's the whistle of the wind.

I peek out through the red-tinted glass window in the front door. The silhouette of a giant maple tree sways against a backdrop of moonlit ocean. Nobody's on the porch or on the sweep of steps leading down to the grassy slope. My ears are playing tricks. Back through the hall I go.

Branches screech against the windows. Somewhere outside, a gate is banging. I tiptoe to the back room. The telephone is plugged into the electrical outlet and doesn't work without power.

I open the fuse box. The fuses are all in place—they're dusty, but not a single one is blown. The power appears to be out all the way down the block. Great. Muffled sounds are still coming from somewhere. I follow the sound down the hall again and stop outside the parlor. Pale light seeps out from under the door. I take a long, deep breath and brace myself. Here goes nothing.

I fling open the door and march into the room. Someone, a woman, is standing in shadowy moonlight—high forehead, flushed cheeks. Blue dress. She's tall and rather striking in appearance. If I'd seen her across a crowded room, she would have stood out as starkly beautiful. A faint aura surrounds her. Goose bumps race along my skin. I'm really hallucinating. Or sleepwalking. Or I never left Auntie's bed. My tongue expands to fill my mouth.

Finally I find my voice. "Who are you? What are you doing here? The store is closed."

She doesn't reply.

"You shouldn't be here," I say. "Have you been here all evening? Were you in here when I locked the store? Are you in the book group?"

The electricity comes back on in an explosion of lights. The woman is gone. One moment she was standing in front of me, but now I'm the only one here. I check down every aisle. The window is locked, and the door is behind me. I must have conjured her from my freaked-out imagination.

On the table is a hardcover book. How could I have missed it before? I pick up a heavy memoir with a frayed jacket and brittle pages, fragile from years of wear. *My Life in Africa*, a memoir by Dr. Connor Hunt.

Connor Hunt.

I open the cover—first edition, published in 1975, when the author was thirty-six years old. The author photo splashed across the back cover nearly makes my heart stop beating. The hair is combed a little differently, and he's in a turtleneck and bell bottoms, but the man looks remarkably similar to the Connor I know. Only this man, the Connor Hunt who wrote this book, would be more than seventy years old by now.

Chapter 20

I'm calling Tony on Auntie's landline, at just past two a.m. "I'm leaving in the morning."

"Jasmine, is that you?" Tony's voice is heavy with sleep. "How did you get my number?"

"It's here, in the office. I'm losing my mind. I need to get in touch with my aunt." I pace in my nightgown and slippers, the lights bright, every bulb turned on. All the electricity in town must be flowing into this house. I'm carrying the memoir.

"You've only been here two days. It's the middle of the night. What's going on?" Tony's voice is sharp now. "Is the house on fire? What happened?"

"The house is still standing. There's something seriously wrong with me, though."

"Do you need an ambulance? Hang up and call 911."

"I thought I heard voices, and then I thought I saw some woman in the parlor. I'm hallucinating."

"Whoa, girl. You've got the third eye. I told you."

"Is there some kind of toxic mold growing in this house? Something that could cause hallucinations?"

"Nothing toxic. Your aunt's been talking to the bookstore spirits for years."

"She didn't tell me that."

"I thought you knew."

"I never believed it was for real. I thought she was just eccentric. She is eccentric."

"And so are you, obviously. How can I help? What can I do for you?"

"I didn't know who else to call. Not my family. They'll think I'm crazy. I am crazy! I need to reach my aunt—"

"I can't believe you saw a ghost."

"Not a ghost! I didn't see anyone. I was dreaming. But I found a book." I tell him about the memoir. "It's written by a Dr. Connor Hunt. He looks a little different, not exactly like the Connor I met but very close. Maybe Connor's father. No pictures of any kids—"

"I thought the name sounded familiar. Now I remember. Dr. Hunt, yes. He lived on the island way long ago. Used to go back and forth to Africa. Died there—"

"In Africa? The memoir was published before he died," I say with a shiver. "How did he die?"

"I have no idea."

"It's weird that I would find the memoir sitting out on a

126

table. I don't remember seeing it before tonight. Connor was probably reading it. Or maybe he left it here. It might belong to him. Do we carry copies in the store?"

"I don't know," Tony says. "Your aunt takes in so many books from estates, and only a fraction of the inventory is in the computer system. We have a lot of catching up to do."

"We need to start cataloging the books properly."

"Yeah, okay. Can we talk about this tomorrow? I need to get back to REM sleep."

"I'm sorry. I forgot how late it is."

"No problem. You'd better try to get some shut-eye, too. Make some valerian tea. The stuff stinks, but it works."

When I hang up, I feel no better. I sit in an armchair in the tea room and begin to read the memoir. Through his words, Connor's father returns to life. I absorb his anguish at the limitations he faces in his humanitarian work in Africa. I smell the odors of dust and death, watch children baby-sit cows and snooze on banana boxes. He's forced to work without the simple equipment needed to save people from curable diseases. I take in his bouts with fever, his single-minded dedication to his work, the difficulties of returning to America. The culture shock. He feels responsible for the death of a Nigerian girl who perished from dehydration. He didn't have enough intravenous fluids to treat her. He misses his wife in America. The more I read, the better I know him, and the deeper I fall—into what? Infatuation? Fascination?

Could I feel the same way for Connor? He's not like his father, this serious man who longed to save the world.

Connor seems so laid-back. Does he have noble aspirations? Does he travel to Africa to help people in need? I want to know him better, and I wish I had met his father.

I jolt awake to the shrill ring of the telephone. The book falls off my lap. I must have dozed off, sitting up, in my night-gown. I glance at my watch. Six a.m.

It's Ma, her voice tense with worry. "I'm sorry to get you up so early."

"I was already up," I say, rubbing my eyes. "Has something happened?"

"I tried to call you during the storm, but of course I couldn't get through. Did a tree fall on the house?"

"What? No." I push my hair out of my face. "Why would a tree fall?"

"Happens in storms all the time, especially around Ruma's place."

"A tree has fallen before?"

"No, but there are many tall trees around, and she hasn't hired an arborist to check on the health of those firs."

I roll my eyes. "Ma, the house is fine."

"Dad wanted to come and get you, but the wind was too strong. Better we all stayed indoors."

"Everything's okay here," I say.

"We should all move to California. I've had enough of this weather." Every few months she threatens to move, but she always stays.

"We get rain in California, too, and mud slides," I say. "And earthquakes, and drought, and Santa Ana winds."

"Not these storms. But this is not why I'm calling. I've just heard from your auntie Charu. Sanchita is missing." My mother says this with expectation, as if I'm supposed to instantly solve the problem before the sun rises.

"Missing from where? What happened?"

"She walked out on Mohan. Everyone's distraught. Mohan is beside himself. Have you seen her?" Ma asks, an edge in her voice.

"Why would I have seen her? I barely know her."

"You grew up with her."

I pace, pressing the cordless receiver to my ear. My stomach is growling and I need to pee. "Not exactly. We were forced together during all the parties you guys had when we were growing up. But Sanchita and I never had much in common."

"Perhaps you can get to know each other again, when she returns. Now that you're here. I'm sure she would love to see you. She seems lonely—"

"She has kids, a husband, and a demanding career. She doesn't need me to be her friend. . . ."

"We've got to find her."

"It's early morning. Maybe she left for work. Did Mohan try her office? The hospital?"

"Her overnight bag is gone. She left a note saying she's all right and not to worry, but of course everyone's worried. Mohan's been calling all her friends and her office. She hasn't shown up at work. She hasn't answered her cell phone."

"Maybe she doesn't want to talk to anyone."

"He's very worried."

"She's a grown woman."

"But this isn't like her."

"Maybe she needs some time by herself. Sometimes people do unexpected things, things that don't seem like them. She'll come around."

"She left her children with Mohan."

"He can't take care of them?"

"He doesn't know the number of the babysitter."

"Maybe he could take care of his own children," I say, but I have to feel sorry for the man.

"Jasmine."

"Ma, this is none of our business. It's not her parents' business, either."

"They're worried about her."

"She's an adult. She can make her own decisions. It's not as if she's been kidnapped."

Ma is silent a moment. "Let me know if you hear from her."

"I'm sure Sanchita will call home when she's ready." I hang up, unsettled. I picture Sanchita's children—their pudgy fingers, round faces, luminous eyes. She can't have actually left them. She has everything she could ever want, including a perfect career. Isn't it good enough for her? Did she run off with a lover? If her perfect life hasn't made her happy, what hope is there for the rest of us?

She probably went out for a jog. She'll arrive home none the worse for wear, and everyone will have worried for nothing.

But on my way up the stairs, a crumpled page flutters across the landing. A sheet torn or lost. I pick up the paper; it comes from a book titled *How to Leave Everything Behind and Forge a New Identity.*

Chapter 21

I leave the page on the table in the foyer, bundle up, lock the store, and head for the beach. Morning sunlight peers through a slash in the clouds. The more I inhale the salty air, the stronger I feel. The wet rooftops perspire in the sudden warmth, giving off sheets of steam.

In the sand, I stop to pick up shells and stones. Their pastel colors, the intricate ridges on the pink cockleshells, comfort me. There is order in the natural world, patterns that calm the mind. I've forgotten my cell phone, and I haven't turned on my netbook.

I worry about Auntie Ruma. I worry about Sanchita's children. She has to come back. Finding that page was a coincidence.

Why would she disappear, leave behind the people she loves? Do Robert and Sanchita have similar DNA, a trait that allows someone to hurt another person, to sever all ties?

We, the jilted, the spurned, are left behind to pick up the pieces, to make a life from what remains.

Halfway down the beach, I spot a graceful heron standing on a rock, motionless. As I watch, my breath taking flight in soft clouds of steam, the beauty of this moment hits me. I am alive, right now, right here, sharing the earth with this heron.

When I return to the store, Tony is in the office, tapping away at the computer keyboard. His fingers fly at top speed. His hair sticks up in a new do, smelling of watermelon spray. "Okay, look. Here's his biography. The senior Dr. Connor Hunt. Not much on Wikipedia about him. He must have been pretty secretive. But there's a picture of him dancing with some villagers in Nigeria—look at that."

I peer at the fuzzy black-and-white photograph. "I hardly recognize him in that weird headdress." But he's got a body to die for, all lean muscle and broad shoulders. I can't believe I'm reacting this way to a man who passed away a long time ago.

"He went native." Tony sits back and crosses his arms over his chest. "No details about how he died, except that it was in Africa. His memoir was popular when it came out, but all editions are out of print now."

"I'll save our copy for Connor Junior," I say. "For when he comes back. He'll probably realize he left it behind and he'll be in first thing today."

I collapse into a chair. I feel suddenly worn out. I tell Tony about Sanchita and the page I found.

"It was a sign from the spirits," he says. "She's gone for good."

"That's crazy," I say.

"Maybe." He taps the keyboard and pulls up a new window. "Or a sign for you. You're supposed to forget the past and move on, eh?"

"Sorry, I have the memory of an elephant."

All morning, I find I'm watching for the younger Connor, a habit that annoys me. I did this with Robert—watched for him late into the night.

Just before eleven o'clock, Mohan steps into the foyer, holding Vishnu's hand. The little boy's eyes are dark ringed, as if he's been crying. Mohan's in a silk suit, hair slicked back, his black Mercedes stopped at the curb, the engine still running. Two dark figures wait inside—perhaps a babysitter and the toddler, Durga.

"Mohan, come in!" I say. "Is Sanchita back?"

He shakes his head, motions toward his son. "His mom is on a short trip," he says extra loudly. "She'll be right back."

I nod knowingly. "How can I help you?"

"Your aunt said you would be running story time while she's gone."

"Story time?"

Tony comes up behind me. "You read to the kids."

"Read?" I say. "I'm no good with kids."

"She'll do it," Tony says.

Mohan's shoulders relax. "Thank you so much. Vishnu likes to listen to stories. I'll be back to get him after my morning surgery."

Before I can ask any more questions, Mohan rushes out to

133

the car, jumps inside, and screeches away. I'm standing in the foyer with a tiny boy—a complete stranger. What does one do with children? Vishnu gazes up at me with obvious skepticism. I'm not used to being scrutinized by a small person who has such a wise face.

"All right, it's just you and me, kid," I tell him. But parents start bringing more children, one by one, until seven little ones have arrived. They're milling about in the parlor. My heartbeat kicks up.

"What are we supposed to read?" I whisper to Vishnu. "I'm supposed to tell a story, right? You've done this before?"

He nods solemnly.

"I thought as much."

I lead him into the children's room and peruse the vast collection of books. I'm unsure where to begin.

"Beatrix Potter?" I say.

He nods.

"Mr. White. E. B. White?"

He nods again. "Sometimes Auntie Chatterji does the rabbit ears." He points to a box under the table.

"What do you mean?"

"She puts on a costume and hops around."

"Hops around?" There is no way I'm hopping around.

"And she wears the bunny tail."

Even less chance of that.

"She makes funny noises like a pig or a dog."

I laugh. "I'm going to read and that's it, okay?"

He nods and sighs.

134

I carry a few books into the parlor. The kids are restless, giggling and chatting, sitting in rows on the carpet with their parents. The sea of faces makes my heart pound. My hands grow clammy. Suddenly I'm seized with stage fright. But I stand up front, by the ceramic fireplace.

The room falls quiet.

"I'm here to take over for my aunt, just for today."

The kids stare at me. A little red-haired boy says, "Where's Auntie Chatterji?"

I'm in the spotlight. My throat goes dry. "She'll be back soon. But not today. All right, then. Let's begin."

I open *The House at Pooh Corner* and begin to read. At first the children are quiet, but gradually, as my voice drones on, they start whispering. They fidget. They sigh. They cough.

I read faster and louder. A boy smacks his lips. Another one says, "I have to pee."

A little girl shouts, "I want Auntie Chatterji!"

My heart twists.

Vishnu is watching me. His lips tremble. His eyes brighten with tears. I want to strangle Sanchita. I want to lift little Vishnu into my arms and comfort him.

"Wait," I say. "Just a minute, okay? Everyone wait here."

The room falls silent. Vishnu sniffs.

I slip into the children's book room. My heart pounds. What am I supposed to do? I have to do something to keep Vishnu from bursting into tears. But what?

I'm good at making presentations to clients. I can stand in front of people and keep them interested. But I spout performance numbers; I use a pointer to highlight graphs and trends.

I need props. I rummage through the box and find a rooster's comb, a silly donkey tail, rabbit ears, and a few hand puppets. What am I going to do with this stuff? I'll figure it out.

I grab a few books off the shelf and drag the box into the parlor, where my audience members are sitting cross-legged and expectant on the carpet. I'll have to improvise.

"All right," I say, standing up front, "I'm going to try again."

Vishnu sniffs. The boys fidget.

I open the silver anniversary edition of *Peter Rabbit*, take a deep breath, and begin to read. " 'Once upon a time there were four little Rabbits, and their names were—Flopsy, Mopsy, Cotton-tail, and Peter.' "

"I love this one!" a little girl shouts. Her blond curls bounce.

To my surprise, a warm feeling seeps through me. " 'They lived with their Mother in a sand-bank, underneath the root of a very big fir-tree.' "

My voice slides across the room, mesmerizing the children. This deceptively simple, seemingly benign story of an adventurous rabbit hides an underlying horror. The evil human, Mr. McGregor, captured Peter Rabbit's father and killed him. Mrs. McGregor cooked him in a pie. Peter slips into McGregor's garden, gorges on vegetables, and narrowly escapes his father's sad fate.

As I read, I put on the costumes and act out the parts. Part of me watches from a distance. I should feel silly or humiliated, but the rabbit ears fit perfectly, and the more I act, the more the children laugh. I hop around the room. The kids roar with laughter. And Vishnu's eyes change. They fill with the light of imagination. I'm someone new, someone I've never been, or perhaps someone I've always been.

Chapter 22

After story time, the parents come up to thank me. "They hardly ever sit still for that long," one mother says. "You're good at this."

"I've had practice. I give presentations at work," I say.

"I see." She gives me a funny look.

The families file out, and finally only Vishnu remains, quietly reading in the children's book room. Mohan shows up half an hour late. "Sorry—surgery went overtime."

"Baba," Vishnu says, tugging his hand, "she read *Peter Rabbit*. And it was fun!"

"Did she?" He smiles at me and mouths the words *thank you* before whisking Vishnu out to the car.

I return the props and books to the children's book room. My chest fills with an odd sense of accomplishment, although all I did was hop around and read to little kids. I didn't snag the Hoffman account or perform any great feat of heroism.

"Lovely reading," a watery voice says behind me. I turn to find an elderly woman in an old-fashioned dress and black hat standing in front of me, holding a fluffy white cat in her arms.

"I didn't hear you come in," I say. The scents of soil, clean air, and something sweet and floral waft into my nose.

"I've always been here." She pets the purring cat in her arms. "My animals come with me. I love them all—dogs, cats, squirrels. I have four thousand acres preserved for the wildlife and of course my Herdwick sheep, all twenty-five thousand of them now."

"Who are you?" She looks strangely familiar.

She pulls a biography off the shelf and shows me the picture on the back cover.

"Looks like a younger version of you," I say.

"I would prefer to appear younger, but I grew old. Ah, well."

"But you can't be Beatrix Potter. Are you a relation, a descendant?"

"I am Beatrix." She lets the cat down, and the fluffy white creature trots to the bookcase, rounds the corner, and is gone. I blink, not believing my eyes.

"This teasing has gone far enough," I say. "Did Tony put you up to this?"

She takes my hand. Her fingers are warm and firm. "The children loved story time."

I let go of her hand and step backward toward the door. "I'm glad they did. I had to make Vishnu smile. His mom will be back soon, and his life will go back to normal."

"Life will never go back to normal. Not now that you've worn the bunny ears." Beatrix smiles. Is she talking about me or Vishnu?

"Jasmine!" Tony is calling, coming down the hall. He pokes his head in the door. "There you are." He pays no attention to the woman in the old-fashioned clothes. "Ruma's on the phone!"

I turn back, but the woman is gone.

I rush out to take the call.

Auntie sounds distant but exuberant. "My dearest niece!"

"How are you? Where are you?" I carry the phone around the corner, into the hall, for a little privacy. "How is your heart? Have you seen the doctor?"

"Don't worry about me. How is life in the bookstore? How do you like my lovely apartment?"

"Oh, Auntie. Why didn't you tell me about the weird things that happen here?" I pace with the phone pressed to my ear. "Why didn't you pay your bills?"

"Isn't Tony helping? If not, I'll speak to him. Hang on." Over the phone, I hear the blare of horns and a man yelling in Bengali.

"Auntie, why did you think I was the only one who could take care of the store while you were away?"

"Because it is true." Auntie covers the receiver and yells for a rickshaw. Then she comes on the line again. "I must go. You must follow your heart. We're all part of something bigger than ourselves. Oh, dear, we're heading off to catch the train to Agra. We're sightseeing."

"We? Who are we?"

"We're visiting the Taj. I haven't been there in years!"

I lose the signal. "Damn it." I slam the receiver back into its cradle.

"You always did like to swear," a familiar voice says behind me.

Robert.

My body betrays me, still responding to him out of habit, alert to the smooth timbre of his voice. "What the hell are you doing here? How did you find me?"

Chapter 23

"Didn't you get my messages?" Robert strides toward me in a black trench coat, his features placed by a careful god in perfect proportion, except for the dent on his nose, just above the bridge, where he tripped and fell on a tree root while running on the track team in high school. He still has a runner's physique, a bounce in his stride as if he might break into a sprint.

"I don't get a good signal here." I need a paper bag or I'm going to hyperventilate. Or throw up. I can't decide.

"You're a hard woman to track down, but Scott Taylor gave me the tip I needed. I have to talk to you." His eyes, a mixture of hazel and gray, have always looked deceptively benevolent. I wonder when Lauren will understand his true character.

"I'm working," I say. "Talk to my lawyer." I gather up an

armful of books. I don't know what to do with them. Where is Tony when I need him?

"I'd like to talk to you in person."

"Where is Lauren? Does she know you're here?" I can't help the nasty tone in my voice as I say Lauren's name.

"She knows. Is there a place we can go?" Robert looks around as if trying to find a clear space in the clutter.

"You've had months to talk to me. I said no, I'm not selling the condo for such a low price."

"That's what I want to discuss. The condo."

"What else is there to say? Talk to the real estate agent."

"I need to discuss this with you."

I drop the books on a table. "Why? I'll see you at the final settlement hearing next month."

"I came all the way up here to see you. Can't you be civil?"

Customers are starting to look at us. "Outside," I whisper. "Not in here."

A few minutes later, I'm hurrying up the block, the wind whipping my hair into my face, Robert hunched beside me, keeping pace. "Why the rush?"

"Don't ever show up without warning me again. Scratch that. Don't ever show up. Period."

"I know you're angry with me."

"Angry doesn't begin to describe what I feel."

"I tried to reach you. I wanted to see you. Are you okay? I still worry about you."

"You worry about me?" But my heart softens by a micron.

For an instant, I flash back to our romantic walks together. We were like this, nearly shoulder to shoulder, discussing retirement, the future, the places we wanted to travel.

"You didn't tell me you were leaving L.A."

"I don't have to tell you anything," I say, but I'm a little sorry for him. His nose is pink from the cold. He's fragile in this kind of weather, and I'm not.

"Can we go inside? Maybe here?" He turns into Le Pichet, a dimly lit French restaurant. A voluptuous waitress leads us to a corner table in the shadows. A romantic table, as if we're a couple.

"May I bring you drinks?" she says.

"Water for me," I say.

I watch Robert. He keeps his gaze above her neckline. He's trying. "I'll have something hot. Coffee."

She nods and walks away. Robert does not watch her go. He keeps his eyes on me.

I fold my arms across my chest for protection. "You have five minutes. Start talking." I'm barely aware of the buzz of conversation, the clinking of glasses, the smells of onion and wine.

"I can't drink my coffee in five minutes." Robert fixes his gaze on my forehead, as always. That should have been a sign, his inability to look me in the eyes.

The waitress brings my water and Robert's coffee. "Menus?" she says.

I shake my head.

She nods and walks away.

Robert drinks his coffee black as always. He still gulps instead of sipping. He still has a habit of clearing his throat.

"You missed a spot again," I say, pointing to the left side of his jaw, just below his ear. Even in this dim light, I can see his mistakes. He was never careful about shaving, although he was always careful about keeping secrets.

"You look good," he says, unfazed by my comment. "Something about you is different. Did you lose weight? Or is it your hair?"

I touch my wild locks self-consciously. Robert always made me aware of my appearance. "What about the condo?" I say. "Let's stay on point."

"Can't I at least tell you you're beautiful?"

"Not anymore." With every word, he carves a hollow space inside me. I imagine him on his knees, begging my forgiveness. *I loved you all along. How could I have thrown away those mornings in the sun, making love on the living room carpet, frying mushroom omelets? I don't love Lauren. I love you. I want to live with you happily ever after. . . .*

My heart will leap and then break into a thousand pieces again. I will say . . . *I loved you. I'm falling apart. I wanted those things, but now there's no going back. How could you do this to me?* I'm at the edge of a precipice.

"Could you take a look at this?" He pulls a sheaf of folded papers from an inside pocket of his jacket, like a magician, and slides it across the table. The pages are stapled together.

"What is this?"

His gaze softens. "Take a look. Please."

I unfold the paper. On the top page:

THE GRANTOR(S), Jasmine Mistry, for and in consideration of: One dollar and love and affection conveys and quitclaims to the GRANTEE(S), Robert Mahaffey, Jr., the following described real estate, situated in the County of . . .

The colors leach from the room. The bartender, the couples huddled at tables, the hanging plants—everything darkens to black and gray.

"You want me to give up my rights to the condo," I say. "But we agreed to sell it together." This is the last thing we were to do as a couple. The last thing.

He clasps his hands in front of him on the table. Pretty hands, long fingers. Hands I once held with trust. No ring on his wedding finger.

I look away. I. Feel. Nothing.

"I wanted to sell," he says. "It's not me. It's Lauren."

I push my chair back, to put more distance between Robert and me. He suddenly smells foul, despite his usual subtle cologne, that familiar mineral scent.

"She wants to live in the condo." In the middle of all those memories. "She loves the light, the windows."

"She wants to take over my house."

"Not strictly yours," he says. "Ours. And we—Lauren and I—want to know if you're willing to give it up, out of the goodness of your heart." He sits back and shoves his hands in the pockets of his coat.

"Out of the goodness of . . . ? What?" I chuckle, softly at first, then louder. A woman at a nearby table glances over at me. Robert's face reddens. I throw the paper across the table at him. "Nice try, Robert. I won't give up my home to that woman. How could you ask me to? How could you ask me to give up everything I put into that place? All the love, the blood, the sweat? The memories? The tears? How could you ask such a thing?" Even as I say this, I understand how cold Robert can be. Until now, I couldn't face the depth of his indifference.

"I didn't think you'd go for it," he says. "But I promised Lauren I would give it a try."

"You promised her." My voice is rising. "How much more hell can you put me through? Is it not enough that I gave up nearly everything I own—cleaned out my savings—to pay my damned legal bills? Now you had to follow me to the ends of the earth." I get up, nearly knocking over my chair.

"Jasmine, please. Don't be so angry with me. I've told you so many times, I'm sorry. I'm so, so sorry." He reaches out and rests his hand on mine, so quickly that I can't pull away fast enough. His touch is a painful sting.

"Robert, don't come here again. Don't call me."

"Just a minute. Wait." He grabs my wrist. "Sit down. Just one more minute."

I yank my arm away. "Don't touch me. I'm leaving."

"You didn't look at the other pages. We're offering

another option. We're willing to buy you out, buy out your share of what the condo is worth. Here." He flips a few pages and shows me a highlighted paragraph.

This can't be happening. This isn't real. I see Robert, dressed for our wedding, slipping the ring on my finger. Robert, holding me close, in the crook of his shoulder. Robert, feeding me ice cream from a spoon.

"That amount?" I say mechanically, staring at the paper. "My share is worth much more than that. No, I won't do it."

"Jasmine."

I'm already rushing to the door. Robert scrambles to pay for his coffee. I'm racing down the street. The wind howls, and driving rain smacks me in the face.

"Jasmine, wait!" He's close behind me.

"No, Robert." When I reach the door to the bookstore, I'm soaked to the bone. My teeth are chattering. I'm shaking all over. "I won't give up the condo," I say, breathless. "I loved that place. That was our home, not hers. We're selling, Robert. You should not have come here. Find yourself another place to live. Don't ever talk to me again. From now on, speak to my lawyer."

"You never gave an inch," he says.

I stumble inside, slam the door in his face, turn the deadbolt. Then I rest my back against the door, slide down to the floor, and burst into tears.

Chapter 24

Tony directs me to sit in a saggy armchair and makes me a cup of chamomile tea. Customers glance at me with concern. He ushers everyone out of the room.

I grip the mug in both hands, savoring the warmth. "Thank you, Tony. I needed this."

"In my opinion, no selfish bastard is worth the tears," he says. "The minute he walked in here, I knew he was trouble."

"I wish I had known before I married him. I can't believe I considered staying with him."

Tony grabs a damp rag and wipes down the counters. He's obsessively neat, but somehow he can't keep up with Auntie Ruma's clutter. "You mean after you found out . . . ?"

"I read about surviving infidelity. I thought—maybe I can make this work. Maybe he cheated because I was boring—"

"You're wound up, but you're not boring. Don't ever think of yourself that way."

"Thanks, Tony. You're kind, you know that?"

"Hey, what can I say? Maybe he's going through the midlife crisis thing."

I grip the mug tighter until I'm sure it might break. "I thought of that. I thought maybe he needed more attention or I was unavailable. I don't know why he didn't just leave. I don't know what would have hurt more."

Tony squeezes the rag in the sink and drapes it across the faucet. "What a lowlife for cheating on you."

I sip the soothing liquid. A few chamomile leaves have broken free of the tea bag and are floating to the top of the cup. "He's narcissistic, totally self-involved. . . ." My hands tremble so much I spill the last of my tea on my lap. I jump to my feet, and Tony is there in a second, wiping at my jeans with the rag.

"You're going to be okay. Deep breaths. You have to believe in yourself. You're a survivor."

My throat tightens, and tears sting my eyes again. "I feel like a wreck, and we've been separated almost a year—"

"Takes time. You'll feel better. Go and do something fun. Bungee jumping. Cliff diving."

"I'm sad, not suicidal." I wipe my cheeks. Black mascara comes off on my fingers. "I want time to leap forward, past all this pain. I don't want to go through this."

"I've heard time travel may be possible someday, but for now, you need to let it out. Scream and yell."

"I don't want to scream and yell. I'm okay now. I'm going to put some books away." I leave my empty cup on the counter and stride down the hall, my chin up. In the Self-Help section, a bunch of used paperbacks are piled in a corner. *The Woman Alone, Private Lies, First Aid for the Betrayed.* . . .

I pick up one book, then another, and throw them against the wall. Each one hits with a thud and tumbles to the floor. The only other person in here, a round woman in a purple bonnet, gives me a startled look and hurries out of the room.

I keep throwing books, and the more I throw, the better I feel. At the bottom of the pile is the book *How to Be a Better Wife.*

I stare at the book for a moment, my mind blank. Then I rip off the cover and begin tearing out the pages, one by one, then in handfuls. Yes, take that. Here's what a good wife does.

Chapter 25

"This one is *so beautiful*," Gita says in a breathless voice. She unfolds the red sari on the glass countertop of Krishna's Indian Fabrics in Bellevue. We've been shopping all morning, traipsing around every sari store within an hour's drive of Seattle.

"Looks like blood to me," I say. "So bright, like a bloodred stoplight." My head still aches from my encounter with Robert yesterday. Did he stay in a fancy Seattle hotel, or did he hop a flight back to L.A., to Lauren? *You never gave an inch,* he said. What was that supposed to mean?

"This doesn't look like blood at all," Gita says, frowning at me. "Or a traffic light. Reminds me of roses! A bouquet of flowers. I love this one."

"Whatever you say. You wanted my opinion—"

"Don't you love the gold border?"

"It's printed, not woven," Ma says.

"But the print is beautiful. You're both against me!"

"Don't you want a properly woven border?" Ma says.

Gita pouts, picks up another red sari, discards it.

On the drive over, she didn't stop talking about the wedding—what type of paper to use for the invitations, what flowers to order, what color the tablecloths should be. I worried about all the same things before my wedding—about details that, in the end, didn't matter.

"This one isn't silk," Ma says, rubbing a pink sari between her fingers.

The woman behind the counter, a pudgy, creamy-skinned beauty in a banana-colored sari and copious costume jewelry, waves her hand. "Chiffon is all the craze," she says.

"Chiffon's fine. I don't care if it's silk or not." Gita holds the sari up to the light. The material is translucent, X-rated if she wears nothing underneath. "I love the way it looks and feels. A possibility, right? Will Dilip find me ravishing?"

"He'll find you looking like bubble gum," Ma says. "Too pink."

The smells in here—of spice and fabric and body odor— are making me nauseous. Half the store is an Indian grocery. The imported clothes are squished into the other side, where customers mill about, pulling *salwar kameezes* off racks, trying on cotton *kurtas*, shawls, and piles of saris.

"One looks like blood, the other's too pink," Gita says. "I'm glad you two aren't choosing for me."

"We're trying to help you," I say. "Do you want us to lie?"

Gita glares at me. "I want you to be totally honest."

Then don't get married. Don't worry about saris. In the end, the rituals don't matter. But I force a smile. I don't want to dampen Gita's exuberance.

Ma pulls another sari from the pile on the counter. "How about this one? Darker red and such a lovely silk."

"Too dark," Gita says.

The banana-clad woman produces more saris from the shelves behind her, dropping them on the counter while she keeps her gaze focused on some young girls giggling in a back corner, pasting sparkling round *bindis* on their foreheads.

"What about wearing another color?" Ma says. "Blue or green or—"

"If I'm going to wear a sari, I should wear red," Gita says, sifting through the samples on the counter. "Isn't that what a Bengali bride wears?"

"You can choose what you want," Ma says. "I thought you were blending East and West."

"We are—but Dilip's family might want me to wear traditional red."

Ma unrolls a silver sari with a striking red border. "What matters is what you want."

I'm surprised to hear my mother say this. Perhaps she'll allow this much, for Gita to choose her own wedding sari, now that she's marrying an Indian.

"I'm not sure what I want," Gita says. "But you're right, I shouldn't compromise." She motions to the banana-clad woman. "Do you have more silk saris with woven borders?"

The woman nods her head sideways and produces another stack of saris in various colors.

"Why are you bothering to look here at all?" I say. My feet are starting to hurt. I'm ready for lunch. We've been shopping for three hours at three different shops, unfolding saris and holding them up to the light. I'm tired of all the gaudy costume jewelry.

"I need to take my time," Gita says. "The wedding has to be perfect."

"If you expect nothing to go wrong, you'll be disappointed," I say. "Remember the photographer was late to my wedding? Then he took too long to send me the pictures. . . ." Doesn't matter anymore.

Ma and Gita are quiet for an awkward moment, then Gita smiles. "I can do my best."

Ma lays out a green sari on the counter, imprinted with giant lotus flowers. "Now this one is lovely!"

"No!" Gita says. "I'll look like a frog in a lily pond."

The banana-clad woman moves away to help a customer who is pointing at the Light and Lovely skin-bleaching cream under the glass. For Indians, pale skin is still considered beautiful. My fading Los Angeles tan would not qualify.

I can't believe the colors of some of these saris—neon lime, lemon yellow. "Auntie Ruma is bringing you saris from India," I say. "I'm sure they'll be higher quality."

"Why can't I look here? There's a silk sari, and another one, and another one. They're beautiful."

"You could wear what you're wearing now," I say, pointing

at Gita's simple white dress, which she wears beneath a long, button-down blue sweater. "You look elegant."

"I can't wear white at a Bengali wedding!" She screws up her perfect nose. "The color of mourning?"

"You can wear any color you want. A wedding is just a ceremony; overrated, if you ask me. We put so much emphasis on the ritual but what really matters is the character of the person you're marrying. Is Dilip going to sleep around on you? That's what you should ask yourself."

"Jasmine!" Ma says.

"Sorry—I couldn't help it."

Gita's lips tremble. "Don't ruin this for me, Jasmine."

I hold up my hands. "I didn't mean it. I just worry about you. I want you to be okay. I want you to be ready for this."

"I am ready. Stop worrying about me. Dilip and I are going to live happily ever after."

"Okay, then, I'm happy for you."

"You don't sound happy. You're not, are you? You're bitter."

"Girls!" Ma yells. She unrolls a bright orange sari and waves the fabric in the air between Gita and me, like a peace flag. "How about this one? It's silk, lovely."

"Ma, no!" Gita stamps her foot on the floor, something I haven't seen her do since she was a child throwing a tantrum. "The Hare Krishnas wear orange. They're a cult!"

Ma rolls up the sari again. "How was I supposed to know? I don't want you two arguing like children."

"We're not arguing," Gita says, glaring at me. "Jasmine thinks it's a waste of time to shop for a sari."

"I didn't say that. Just be careful. Just be . . . sure. Do you want to be with the same man, day in and day out, committed to him? Your finances entangled with him? You might even have children before you find out you're not right for each other, and then what?"

"I'm as sure as I'll ever be." Gita ignores my advice, as usual. She is starry-eyed, blindly in love. The brightness of her idealism could illuminate a planet. The trouble is, the light can't last.

I'm back in the bookstore by closing time, after a day of shopping, arguing, and trying various sweets and pastries at the Indian bakery in Bellevue—so Gita can choose her dessert menu for the wedding. I did my best to be helpful. I did my best to be happy for Gita.

Tony left me a note, wishing me a wonderful weekend. I collapse into an armchair with a cup of tea, propping my feet on an ottoman. Auntie's books don't argue, they don't make demands, they don't talk back. They don't remind me of things I'd rather forget. I'm strangely comforted here, in the chaotic clutter and dust, even if my nose is itchy.

"Jasmine," someone says behind me. A baritone voice. I turn around in my chair. He looks stunning against a faint backdrop of light, raindrops glistening on his windbreaker. He carries his usual scent of the outdoors, of salty air fresh from the ocean. "Connor!" I say, sitting up straight. I completely forgot our date.

Chapter 26

"You forgot." He leans casually against the doorjamb.

"Oh. My. I did." I get up quickly, brush down my jeans, pat my tangled hair.

"I can come back another time." His voice, several tones lower than Robert's, has a strange effect on my nerve endings.

"I'm sorry. I've been . . . A lot has happened." I'm suddenly aware of my wrinkled shirt, puffy eyes. I'm blushing.

"Long week, huh?" His voice resonates, and my heart beats crazily. He glances at his watch, the same old silver chronograph with the leather strap.

"My ex-husband asked me to give up my home to him and his new girlfriend—"

"Ouch—that bites. Your ex is a dipstick."

An expression from the past. But I like it. "Should I have said yes? I mean, am I selfish for trying to hold on to that place, or at least get the amount I deserve from the sale?" I'm talking half to myself, but Connor is listening intently.

"I'm sorry you're losing a home that meant so much to you," he says gently.

Suddenly I can hardly breathe. The tears are rising all over again. "And my sister is getting married. I spent all day with her and my mother, shopping for wedding saris."

"A wedding. Wow. Sad occasion."

I wipe my damp eyes. "I know weddings are supposed to be joyful, but I'm divorced. I guess I'm sad."

"It's okay to be sad. I've had many sad moments of my own."

"Oh? Were you married?"

"Once, a long time ago. Seems like another life."

"What happened? Were you divorced?"

He frowns briefly. "She passed away." His tone is tight, final.

"I'm sorry."

He nods slightly, and I decide not to press. I pretend to pick lint off my shirt. "I'm a wreck. I must look awful."

"No, you're beautiful." Somehow, when he says this, I feel beautiful, too. "I've been looking forward to seeing you all week."

"I wasn't sure you would come." My fingers are trembling, my heart racing. My body is embarking on a journey of its own. I clasp my hands together in front of me. "I should go upstairs and change—"

"I don't want to let you out of my sight."

I blush. "Um, okay. What do you want to do?"

He rubs his finger across his eyebrow, his trademark move when he's stumped or thinking. "How about a tour of the house? This place is historic. Drafts and all. Then I could make you dinner."

"You don't have to—"

"I want to."

"Okay, a tour." I try to remember what Auntie told me about the house, over the years, in bits and pieces. "Originally, I think this place belonged to the Walker Timber Company. But that was a century ago."

He presses his large hand to the ornate banister. "The elegant construction, it's—"

"Queen Anne style. The Walker family sold the place in the early nineteen hundreds, I think, when the timber industry went downhill. The house passed through maybe two other owners—I'm not sure—before my aunt and uncle bought it thirty years ago. They renovated the rooms together. My uncle died nearly a decade ago. Heart attack."

"I'm sorry—your aunt must miss him."

Uncle Sanjoy's kind, round face pops into my mind—his paunch, his perpetually watery eyes. "I miss him, too. He was kind to her. The bookstore was her dream. He was in business. They didn't actually live in this house together. They had a place a few blocks away. She moved in here after he died."

"She never remarried?"

I shake my head.

"She must be lonely."

"She has customers and friends and my parents and Tony. But now she's getting older, and she's not well. She went to India for a heart operation."

"You must be worried about her."

"I am, but she just called to tell me she's okay." I exhale with relief. "There's something else she's not telling me. I can only hope she comes back safe and sound. She loves this old dusty bookstore."

"I don't blame her. The place has charm."

Charm. Maybe it does, a little. "Um, come with me. I'll show you the rest of the house."

I lead him through the rooms, pointing out the old fireplaces, wallpaper, the wainscoting, showing him the different sections of the bookstore.

"*Curious George*," he says, pulling out a yellow picture book in the children's room. "Brings back memories."

"I read that one, too."

We pull out one book after another, reminiscing about the stories of childhood.

"I loved Superman but not the Hardy Boys," he says.

"I read the Hardy Boys but not Nancy Drew. I had a crush on those boys." I pull out an old copy of *What Happened at Midnight.*

"On both of them?"

"Yeah, but not at the same time."

Connor chuckles. He follows me into the Antiquarian room, full of piles of musty volumes crammed together on tall bookshelves.

"My aunt keeps so many old books in here—from the dawn of history."

"She's a collector. Look at this stuff." He pulls out a slim, tattered book. "This one is old. Might fall apart."

He hands me the volume. I hold it carefully in my hands. *Tamerlane and Other Poems*, by "a Bostonian." "No author. Just some Bostonian."

"Keep it," he whispers. "It's my gift to you."

"Your gift?" I say. "But it was here."

"I brought it here, a while ago. I was waiting for someone to find it."

"You put this book on the shelf? Published in 1827." I read the small type on the cover page. "'Young heads are giddy, and young hearts are warm, / And make mistakes for manhood to reform.—Cowen.'"

He looks at me, his eyes dark.

Young hearts are warm. My knees are weak. I'm a walking cliché of giddy. "Words from the past," I say.

Connor grins. "A Bostonian trying to convey a message. Don't lose the book. Keep it in a safe place."

"In the office, then," I say, leading him down the hall. In Auntie's office, I slip the book into my giant handbag. Then I lead him down the hall to the large front staircase. "There are other floors, but we don't have to see them."

"You're not going to invite me up?" He grins, his eyes twinkling with boyish mischief. A tingling sensation rushes through me like a mild electric shock.

"The Metaphysics and Science rooms are on the second

floor, and above that is my aunt's apartment, on the top floor. I'm staying there while she's gone."

He runs his fingers through his hair. "Gonna show me?"

Legs wobbly, I lead him up the wide staircase to the second floor. I show him the books, the old laundry chute, the cubbyholes, the hidden corners in closets.

We're at the door to the narrow staircase. "This route was for the servants. Weird, isn't it? The way they built these houses."

He looks up through the cavernous darkness. His arm brushes mine, sending another tingle through me. "Gothic. And you're staying here alone? You're brave."

"I don't think of myself that way." But maybe I am. Brave. I take a deep breath and climb up.

Chapter 27

Connor Hunt follows me all the way up to the apartment. In Auntie's small living room, his footsteps creak behind me. I hear a faint hum in the air.

"Nice place," he says. "Homey."

"Thanks. All my aunt's doing."

His smell is stronger in here—a kind of woodsy aroma that makes me think of camping. I haven't been camping since childhood. He strides to the window and stoops a bit to see outside. He has a force about him, a kind of simmering masculinity that makes my throat dry.

"Helluva view," he says. "Ferry's on its way in. Come here. Look at the stars."

Should I stand this close to him? A few steps from Auntie's bedroom? I peer out at a thick medley of stars in an oil-black sky. "Wow. In L.A., you can't see the stars anymore.

Not like this. I forgot about this sky—the way it clears up here, the way the rain washes everything away."

"How long have you lived in L.A.?" His arm touches mine. I feel his solidity through the fabric of his shirt.

"Since I left home. Long time ago. I was eighteen. The condo I shared with Robert is on the beach. Beautiful area, but even there, the sky isn't black like this. It's orange at night there."

"Sky-glow. Light pollution. A side effect of industrial civilization."

"Sky-glow. Is that an actual word in the dictionary?"

"It's the combination of all light reflected from what it has illuminated. The light escapes into the sky, and the atmosphere scatters and redirects the light back to the earth."

"So in L.A., I'm seeing sky-glow."

"That's right."

"Is the sky like that in other places? Have you traveled a lot? Maybe to Africa—like your dad?"

He looks down at me, turning his face so that his sil-houette is half illuminated by the moon. In this light, he looks larger than life and more beautiful, too, the shadows and planes of his face sharp and strong. "How did you know about my dad?"

"You left his memoir here. I found it on a table. I saved it for you."

"Ah, I see. Thank you. Yes, I've been to Africa."

"Following in his footsteps. He's quite a man."

He glances at me sharply. "He died over twenty years ago."

"I'm sorry." I touch his arm. "You must miss him."

He stiffens perceptibly. "I was young when he passed away."

I long to ask how his father died in Africa, but I don't want to be rude. "You must have fond memories of him."

"Fond, yes." His voice is distant.

"You must have grown up admiring him. He was fearless and caring and selfless. And so serious about his calling."

"Serious. Yes." He's staring up at the stars.

"If he were alive today, I think I could fall in love with him."

"Love. Really."

"Isn't that crazy? I loved reading about his life. Was Africa different for you? Do you remember going there with him when you were little? Did you go after you grew up?"

He's silent a moment, then: "In some places in Africa, the sky is so dark, the stars so abundant, the universe seems made of them."

"What was most surprising to you? Or unsettling?"

"The extent of suffering. Preventable, treatable pain. Many of the people we saw had never been to a doctor."

"Never?"

"Not once in their lives. Not to a doctor or a dentist. When I went as a physician, I found people with parasites, gum disease—common ailments that had gone untreated for so long, they'd caused other complications. We treated what we could."

"What happened to those people after you left? What did they do?"

"That's a good question. Even with all they go through,

their life has a kind of warm simplicity. Ironically, they seem happier than most people here. They're not inundated with advertising, with reminders of the material things that are supposed to make their lives better."

A winking light moves across the sky, against the stars. A plane. I could hop that plane and hitch a flight to Africa, to a life of happy simplicity.

"What you did was noble," I say. "Rushing off to help people in need. Just like your dad."

"A family tradition, yes."

"Do you wish you could go back?"

"I've done all I can do there." He's looking at me in the darkness, the lines of his face rugged in shadow.

"Maybe you could write your own memoir, like your father did." My words hang in the air, suspended.

"Enough about me," he says finally. "What do you do, when you're not running this bookstore?"

"I manage socially responsible retirement accounts. At least, I hope that's what I'll be doing when I get back to L.A. I might be out of a job, if I don't get a big account, only—"

"Only what?"

I sigh. "I'm scared. There, I said it. I'm scared that I'll mess up."

"Why?"

"Because I won't be putting my heart into it. I'm afraid I'll sound desperate because I am. I need my job."

"You don't sound desperate. You sound undecided. That's different."

I smile at him. "I like that. Undecided."

"You're not planning to stay here?"

I step back, away from the moonlight. "The bookstore is my aunt's labor of love. I'm only here for a break. I'm running away from . . . memories. Then Robert came up here and threw me way off."

"You're still in love with him."

Am I? Robert still dredges up powerful emotions inside me. "I still feel things for him. Good and bad, but mostly bad."

"That's only human. We don't just walk away and wash our hands of people."

"I wish I could. Maybe I'm in disappointment. I'm in denial." All the cobwebs come into focus—the clutter, the shadows, the darkness.

"Divorce is like a death. You have to grieve, and then find a new way forward. Life is messy. I bet that sounds like a cliché."

"Do you ever want to get married again?" I ask.

"I'm moving on to a new kind of life. I'm not sure what's in store or who I will be. I'll know when I get there."

"I'm trying to move on, too. But it's hard. We led such a comfortable life, Robert and I. We bought furniture together. We had an elaborate wedding ceremony. Our families were there. Couples aren't supposed to break up if their families get along. Everything about us was so . . . intertwined."

"You're reinventing yourself. We reinvent ourselves all the time, every minute of every day. You can do it. You can untangle yourself from him."

"But why didn't I see? The signs were all there. Late nights in his office, supposedly grading papers or meeting with students. Phone calls. Excuses. I don't ever want to fall in love again. It hurts too much."

"I was hurt that way, once. No joy without pain and all that. Think about it. Yin and yang. Light and dark. Life and death. Love and grief. You're grieving."

When I speak, my voice comes out low and hoarse. "I didn't realize that was what I was doing. I find grief . . . unbearable. I feel as though I wasted six years of my life with Robert. Seven, if you count the year before we were married. I should have known about his affairs."

"He probably went to great lengths to hide them from you."

I wipe a bead of sweat from my forehead. "What was it about me? Was I not good enough for him? Not a good cook? Caught up in my job? Not pretty enough?" *You never gave an inch.*

"You're beautiful and kind and sincere. Who cares if you can't cook? I'll cook for you."

The next sentence catches in my throat. What was I going to say? The heat rises in my cheeks. Why do I have such difficulty breathing when Connor is standing so close? "I shouldn't be telling you all this—"

"I like your candid nature." A bulb winks out in the next room, with a slight crackling sound.

"Being with you is unusual. I feel as though I can say anything, do anything."

"I'm glad. How about supper? Want to watch the chef in action?"

I lead him into Auntie's kitchen, where he glides around, pulling out a cutting board, knife, onion, garlic, and vegetables.

We prepare a stir-fry together in a strange dance, side by side. The room fills with soft vibrations, as if music is playing somewhere beyond our range of hearing. In Auntie's fragrant kitchen, it's as if only the two of us exist.

When we sit at the tiny dining table, he doesn't eat.

"I had dinner before I got here," he says.

"So you're going to watch me eat?"

"With pleasure."

I blush, staring at the steaming, fragrant vegetables on my plate. I begin to eat, and I soon forget to feel self-conscious. The flavors burst forth on my tongue—ginger, garlic, onion, spices. Broccoli and cauliflower have never tasted so good, nor onion so sweet. Connor spins magical tales of his childhood fly-fishing in the rivers of the Olympic foothills, canoeing on pristine lakes. "I've been away a long time, but I'm glad to be back now. The island feels like home."

"Where are you staying?" I ask.

"Fairport Bed and Breakfast, looking for a permanent residence."

"You're going to buy a house here?" I savor a mouthful of mushrooms and onions flavored with ginger.

"I'm a traveler. But I've come full circle now. Back home. I missed this place."

"I missed the island as well," I say, to my surprise. "The beach is soothing. And the moss and the clean air and even the rain." I never thought I would say this.

"Very little has changed. Some of the old restaurants are still here, and shops."

"I used to hike the nature trails, but I haven't done that in years."

"We should explore together," he says. "I haven't seen much since I returned. I've been too busy. My dream was always to open a community clinic here—"

"That's a fabulous idea." Maybe he is like his father, a little.

He moves his chair around the table, next to me, and before I can stop him, he's leaning over to kiss me. His lips are firm, insistent, and I'm transported to a shimmering world of need. An ache of longing spreads through me, but I use all my willpower to extricate myself from his arms.

"I can't do this." I push my chair back and stand. My lips tingle. My body fills with light, as if a universe of stars has come to life inside me.

"Why not?" His eyes are half closed, his face slack.

Every molecule of my body wants to give in, but I can't. "I'm not . . . ready."

"I can wait."

"You might be waiting forever." I put up my inner shield. An image of Robert comes to me. Once, he took my breath away, too.

"Maybe I have forever," Connor says. He gets up slowly, with obvious reluctance, and heads for the door to the stairs.

My heart sinks. "I'll come down with you. Let me put on my shoes."

"No need. I can see myself out. But we've only just started—"

"I need time, Connor. That's all." My heart is hermetically sealed.

"Take all the time you need. But remember, sometimes you have to plunge in, take the risk, grab life with both hands, even if only for a day."

And then he is gone.

Chapter 28

"I'm going to love you forever," Rob whispered on our honeymoon on Maui. His voice flowed across my skin like a tropical aphrodisiac. I lay with my back against him, his arms around me on a gently swinging hammock strung between two palm trees. Maybe we wouldn't go anywhere all day.

We'd rented a sunny cottage on the beach. I could almost believe that this paradise belonged to only the two of us, that there were no other people in the world.

"I'll love you forever and a day." I closed my eyes, felt Rob's chest against my back, his heartbeat, my head in the crook of his shoulder. Pinpricks of sand wafted across my skin. The sea gave off faint smells of salt and seaweed, mixed with Rob's scents of sweat and coconut suntan lotion.

"Forever and two days," he said.

"Three."

"Infinity."

"Infinity plus one."

"No, I mean really love," he said, as if trying to convince himself. Now, I wonder, was he trying to understand what love actually meant, what its limits would be?

"I mean really love, too," I said.

He interlaced his fingers in mine, stroked the palm of my hand with his thumb. "Even when I go bald? When I have to shuffle to the door and my back goes out?"

"We'll shuffle together."

"When I drop my false teeth in a glass every night?"

"Your dad said he still has all his molars—at the reception dinner, remember?"

Rob chuckled. I felt the deep vibrations from his body. "I have no idea how the subject came up. My dad's a hoot."

"Your mom's great, too. I loved her speech at the wedding. All about giving up her son and gaining the daughter she never had—"

"A beautiful daughter." His parents, his two younger brothers, his best friends—the nice people that came with him would also go away with him, eventually. They all belonged in a boxed set.

"Your mom was too generous," I said, my eyes still closed.

"What if I grow a potbelly like that guy over there?" I felt him pointing. I opened my eyes and watched a paunchy sunburned man, wispy gray hairs blowing on top of his head, saunter along the shoreline several yards away. His pale belly spilled over the top of his plaid shorts.

"I don't care what you look like," I said. "I love you for you. For who you are inside."

But what did I truly know of who he was? I thought I understood him, but he projected a false front. How do we really know people?

What do I know of Connor? I pull on my shoes and run downstairs and out the front door, but there's no sign of him. No car, no bike, no man striding away. Only the white ribbon of road winds along the waterfront, and above me, the constellations crowd into a black dome of sky. *Look at the stars.*

Robert never gazed at the stars—he was too busy staring at women. Now I'm free of his earthbound preoccupations, free of the confines of the known world. I imagine soaring through the universe, exploring uncharted territory. I touch my fingers to my lips, where Connor's kiss lingers.

I turn back toward the house, and as I step inside, shivering, his absence closes in around me. Did I make a mistake, sending him away? No, I'm not ready to try again. I may never be ready.

I go to bed, fall in and out of restless sleep, and awaken before the first light of dawn. When darkness begins to lift, I head out to the beach for a jog in the cool morning air, without my cell phone. For now, I need to burn off this frenetic energy.

I follow the shoreline for nearly two hours, until my feet hurt. I half hope to see Connor here, but I find only the cormorants floating on the waves; gulls calling in their piercing voices; and a seal bobbing and dipping, watching me through black marble eyes. I wonder what that seal thinks of me, a wild-haired, lonely woman racing along this windswept stretch of sand?

I stop to gather treasures offered up by the ocean—a ridged pink cockleshell, both halves still intact and connected; clamshells; and colorful volcanic rocks. I return to the bookstore winded but refreshed, just in time for work.

Tony's dressed in lighter blue—faded jeans fashionably ripped at the knees and a pale blue T-shirt that reads *Careful or You'll End Up in My Novel*. He flits about in his usual feverish way, straightening displays and replacing the newspapers in the front hall. "Where did you go? I thought the island swallowed you."

"I was on the beach. Be right back." I run upstairs to shower and dress. I feel alive, alert. The run did me good. I can taste the sea salt on my lips.

Back downstairs, I make a cup of strong coffee and carry a new box of books to the Fiction section.

"How did your date go last night?" Tony asks, coming up next to me. He removes the packing slip from the box.

"He kissed me, that's all."

"What did it feel like?" He grabs books from the box and begins to slip them into new open slots on the shelves.

"Like a kiss. I don't know. Good. It was good."

"Sexy?"

"Yes, that, too." I'm blushing at the memory.

"What else?" Tony sits on the carpet, cross-legged next to the box, and removes the rest of the books in piles.

"Nothing else. We talked." I sit next to him. "I freaked out after he kissed me, and he left. I couldn't help it."

"You're a wounded bird. He'll understand."

"He might be gone for good."

Tony points a book at me. "He'll be back, and next time, have more fun with him."

I give Tony a playful slap in the arm. "I wasn't going to jump into bed right away. What am I supposed to do—take off all my clothes, slip under the covers, and say, 'Here I am, come and get me'?"

"Why not have a little fling? You don't have to marry the guy."

I stare at the novel in my hands. *The Ghost and Mrs. Muir*, about a woman who falls in love with a ghost and waits all her life to be with him. I shove the book onto the shelf. "I'm not ready for that kind of fun."

"You deserve to have that kind of fun. No stress, no crap."

I shelve a copy of *In Love with the Past*. "That's what my ex-husband did, have flings with no stress, no crap. He forgot he had a wife waiting at home. Slight oversight."

"But you're not your ex-husband, and you're no longer married. No Strings Attached can be fun. I'm the king of No Strings Attached. I could give you a few lessons."

I hold up my hand, palm forward. "It's okay. Really. Too much information."

"Imagine, you get to spend time with a hunk of a man who's drooling over you and can give you pleasure. Why not *give in*? Throw all caution to the wind. Then you go back to L.A." He makes a motion as if tossing up dust.

I point to another stack of books. "I'm going to put those away now. And I'll donate the ones we don't need. No more talk about jumping into bed with strange men."

Tony clucks his tongue. "He's not strange. What do you think will happen? You're not going to disappear in a puff of smoke."

"How do you know? Sometimes I feel ephemeral."

"Once you sleep with Connor, you'll feel like a woman again. You'll feel whole."

"I'll feel whole when the divorce is final. I hope Robert doesn't keep trying to take the condo from me."

Tony pats my shoulder. "Look, forget about that guy. Why don't we get out of here for a bit?"

"Who'll keep an eye on the store?" A headache is pushing at my skull again.

"I'll put a Be Right Back sign on the door. We won't get in trouble. I'll take you to the Fairport Café for a cinnamon bun."

"I could use some sugar."

In a few minutes, we're out in the blustery day. The cold air and drizzle feel fresh against my skin.

Fairport Café bustles with local color—students tapping away on computer keyboards, a group of women with their toddlers in strollers. The sweet scents of freshly baked bread and croissants make my mouth water.

"I don't remember so many people living on the island,"

I say. "They look happy." They're so lighthearted, they might float away on the slightest breeze.

"Must be the island's enchantment," Tony says. "Some people think there's magic in the currents that converge around the island; some think it's the weather patterns."

"I need a little happy magic."

We order espresso drinks and two large cinnamon buns from the glass case and sit at a corner table near the window.

I stir my cappuccino. A woman jostles me as she passes with a tray in her hands.

"I wish my aunt would modernize," I say. "I have a feeling she's going to lose the bookstore. I ordered in some new bestsellers, and I dusted. I'm trying, but I can't find all the answers in a month—"

"I'd like someone to give me all the answers, too." Tony slurps the froth from the top of his mocha, leaving a faint white mustache on his upper lip. "Like why I'm not published."

"You're a writer? Your T-shirt gave me a hint."

He sighs and stares into his frothy cup. "I tried to sell exactly fourteen novels, and not one has been published, but I still hold out hope." Through the window, he gazes in wistful yearning at slick raincoats passing in glistening sheets of yellow and blue, as if they are unattainable mirages.

"You're persistent. That's good. I hear you have to hold out a long time in the publishing business."

"I've worked in bookstores for a long time, but your aunt's place is the best. I wouldn't be anywhere else. But I'm waiting for my big break." His voice is full of unfulfilled dreams.

"You could fly to New York and pester a publisher until they accept your manuscript just to get rid of you." I grin, surprised at my own spectacular advice.

"They might report me to the police as a stalker."

"Then stick to the old adage: trust in your talent and never give up."

His face brightens. "I like that one better. You need to do the same."

"I can't trust myself. I chose my ex-husband, after all. I fell for his charm and didn't see what was behind it."

"I'm sorry. I've been through it. Not divorce, but heartbreak. Same thing, right? You feel like you're wandering in a daze."

After Robert left, the world swooped past me while I plodded along, heavy as stone, barely surviving each day. "I went crazy at first, when my husband moved out. I drove away from the gas station with the pump still attached to the tank; I forgot my coffee cup on top of the car, even accidentally wore two different shoes to work."

Tony tears off a sticky piece of cinnamon bun, shoves it in his mouth, and talks while chewing. "How different were the two shoes? Were they, like, one red shoe and one white shoe? A pump and a flat? Come on, be specific."

I laugh, nearly snorting my coffee out my nose. "Two black shoes that looked similar, but one had a strap on the front and the other didn't."

"So it was an honest mistake."

I nod. "But other mistakes were just . . . klutzy. I forgot

to pay the energy bill. I got home one night and the power was out."

"Give yourself a break. You loved the guy, what's-his-name."

"Robert." It comforts me to know that Tony finds the name forgettable.

"Whatever. You wanted to believe the best about him. I know what that's like. I fell in love once. Head over heels."

"Wait, I thought you were the king of No Strings."

He hangs his head, then looks up at me with a sheepish grin. "This one had strings all over it. I would've thrown everything away for love, that one time. My mind was mush." He presses a finger to his forehead. I can't tell whether he's pointing to illustrate his words or pretending to shoot himself in the head.

"What happened?"

He drops his hand to the table, plays with the wooden coffee stirring stick. "I wasn't the one who ended it. I fell in love, and then he cut all the strings, and there wasn't a damned thing I could do." He points the stirring stick at me. "That was when I went crazy. I ran down the street in my underwear, chasing his black Mercedes."

My jaw drops open. "You did what?"

"Middle of the city, morning commute traffic. Everyone got a good look at my Calvin Klein undies. Or were they Ralph Lauren? I don't remember, but who cares? They were briefs, not boxers."

"I'm sorry you had to go through that."

"I wouldn't have thought I would ever do anything like

that, but I was desperate. We do crazy things when we're desperate."

"Yes, we do." *Like fall for a rugged but gentle doctor when you're still getting over your ex-husband.* But I'm smiling a little as I imagine Tony, with his coiffed hair, running down the street in his designer underpants.

"I wish I could fall in love again," he says wistfully. "If you don't want Connor, can I have him?"

"You bum!"

"Okay, I'll wait until you're done with him. First, you have to let him ravish you. You're already different, since you met him. More relaxed, more . . . in your element. And you're not sneezing."

I press a finger to the bridge of my nose. My sinuses are clear. "I haven't taken an allergy pill since—I don't know when."

He points his stirring stick at me again. "Since Dr. Hunt kissed you. See what I mean? There you go."

Chapter 29

Back at the bookstore, I glance at my face in the restroom mirror downstairs. My cheeks are flushed. My eyes are no longer so puffy, and my hair looks darker. Fewer gray strands sprout at my temples.

"Maybe it's the kiss," I say to my reflection. "Or maybe it's because I'm reading *Winnie the Pooh* again. Go figure."

When I step out of the bathroom, I glimpse a little boy wandering into the children's book room, his mess of hair like a pile of wet straw. Perched on his nose is an enormous pair of glasses that make his eyes appear unnaturally big. He bends his head forward, nearly resting his chin on his chest, as if the weight of the glasses is all too much for his head. On his back, an enormous blue, lumpy backpack protrudes like a grotesque growth. He's in a miniature gray suit jacket, plaid sweater underneath, with a red tie tucked inside, jeans, and brown penny loafers. He stares at the floor, his hand gripping the straps of his backpack.

"May I help you?" I ask him. "Are you looking for a book?"

He nods, still staring at the floor.

He does not like to hunt or hurt, he does not play in sand or dirt. . . .

Dr. Seuss, speaking in my head. Must be a memory rising to the surface. "Do you want adventure, to escape to another world?" I ask the boy.

The boy nods, his face lighting up.

The Lion, the Witch and the Wardrobe falls sideways on one of the shelves right at the boy's eye level. He picks up the book, looks at the picture on the cover, and smiles.

I kneel in front of him. "It's a wonderful story, and we have many more."

He smiles, and I see how much courage he gathered to come here. I see how the world appears to him—large and noisy and scary. He is afraid to look anyone in the eye. He's so shy, he crosses to the other side of the street as soon as someone appears in the distance, walking toward him. He doesn't ask for things. He goes without, so he won't have to talk to anyone.

"You can take the book," I say. What am I doing? I'm not helping Auntie's profits.

He smiles as if I've handed him a million dollars. He rummages in his pocket, pulls out a wallet.

I push his hand away. "This one is on me."

"Really?" His smile widens.

"Hold on to your cash."

He is bursting with happiness as he heads for the door, a bounce in his step. His gaze angles a little upward now, not down toward the floor.

In this moment, I don't want to be anywhere else, doing anything else, even when a young woman wanders into the parlor, crying, and stands in front of the Grief and Recovery shelf.

"Are you all right?" I ask. "Did you lose someone?"

"How can you know that?"

Good question. "I just figured. You look sad."

Tears slip from the corners of her eyes. She holds a paperback, *Surviving Pet Loss.* She wipes her cheeks, her lips trembling. "I'm Olivia."

"Jasmine. The book you're holding—"

"Pets this, pets that. He wasn't my pet. He was my muse, my soul mate. I don't know what I'll do without him." Her voice shakes. She needs something, anything to grasp on to. "I remember every detail. He used to wake me with a paw on my cheek. So gentle. He curled up in my lap and rested his chin on my wrist. He was the most magnificent, fluffy tabby. He used to squint up at me with such love and trust." She sniffs, breaks into sobs.

"You came to the right place." My voice is thick with emotion.

"Sometimes it's nearly impossible to go on." Olivia presses her hand to her chest. A tear hovers on her eyelash, catching the light. "When I remember he's gone, my sweet little fur boy, it's like someone is dropping a house on my heart. But nobody understands, because he wasn't human."

"I'm so sorry. You'll always miss him, but there will be hope." I want to tell her I understand loss. The death of dreams, of shared daily habits, of comfort.

"Thank you," she says. "I hope you're right."

My gaze is drawn to the shelves. A book glows in a direct shaft of sunlight. Just as the mango book was illuminated when Professor Avery came in. Only I ignored the light then.

I pull out the book, a tattered hardcover with a drawing of a ragged-eared cat on the front. I hand the book to her.

"*The Fur Person*, by May Sarton," she reads softly. "My Taz was a fur person, too. In his eyes, I saw the soul of a little old man." She reads the first page. "This cat lived with her years ago. They're both long dead now."

"But he was alive once, experiencing the world," I say. "Now, through her words, he's immortal."

"I wish Taz could have lived forever. His playmate, Molly, misses him. She's a calico cat." Olivia is quiet a moment. "Do you have animals?" She looks at me sharply, as if my answer will be the measure of my soul.

"Well, uh, I'm pretty busy these days." I feel a strange pang in my chest, longing for a soul mate like Taz. "I had a cat once, Willow. She lived seventeen years. I would've liked another cat, but I left for college, and then . . . My ex-husband was allergic."

"Which is why he's your *ex*."

"Exactly." Until now, I've focused on what I miss about Robert, not on the restrictions he imposed on my life.

Olivia throws her arms around my neck. "Thank you for helping me find this book."

"It was just . . . there."

"No, you helped." She steps back, holding the paperback close to her chest. "It's good to know someone else loved her cat enough to write his story. This bookstore could use a cat, don't you think? Bookstores are supposed to have resident felines."

"That's up to my aunt."

Olivia hands me a business card. "This is where I work. Come in anytime. I'm sure your aunt would love a cat."

The card reads, *Meow City. A No-Kill Cat Sanctuary. Fairport, WA.* I tuck the card into the back pocket of my jeans. "Thanks, I'll think about it."

On her way out of the store, she turns to look over her shoulder. "Don't think too long."

Chapter 30

I watch Olivia walk along the block and disappear around the corner, her head down as she reads.

"What's the title?" a teenage girl is saying to her friend as they stride past me in the hall.

"I forgot my book list for the stupid assignment," the other girl says. They're both dressed in black, wearing eyeliner so thick, they look dead. "It's about some old guy who wants to catch a giant fish. I mean, how boring. And then he kills it, even though he calls it his brother. Come on, who would kill their brother? Totally lame."

"Yeah, lame-o-rama," the other girl says.

I clear my throat. "Um, I bet you're looking for *The Old Man and the Sea* by Ernest Hemingway." How could I remember such a detail? I must have read the book in high school.

The girls stare at me as if I have a large blemish on my nose, but they buy two copies of the vintage paperback before leaving the store. Now they'll have to read the book, no excuses.

I managed to open most of the windows, clear a few aisles, dust tables and shelves, and bring in more light. As the days pass, I fall into a rhythm, jogging on the beach in the mornings, visiting my parents, helping Gita make wedding arrangements. Each conversation brings back a painful memory, but I don't complain. Gita deserves these fleeting moments of happiness.

I keep hoping to see a hint of Connor. I find I'm watching for him, spinning around when I feel a breath on my neck, jumping when the telephone rings.

The next Thursday morning, Auntie Ruma calls again.

"Auntie, you haven't called in a week. I was worried about you."

She sounds distant and perky. "My heart has been fixed, once and for all." I can tell by her voice that she's smiling.

I mouth a silent prayer of thanks. "I'm so glad. When did you have the procedure?"

"Procedure, ah, yes. Few days back." I hear conversation and commotion in the background.

"What's going on there? Where are you?"

"Just preparing for a little travel."

"Are you well enough? Are you in the hospital?"

"Of course not. I'm quite well." She sounds far away.

"Who's taking care of you? Are you in Kolkata?"

"So many questions. I'll tell you all, in time. For now, I'm safe and happy. You must keep my secret, nah?"

"I hope you know what you're doing. Do you have a telephone number? When will you be back?"

"On schedule. Two weeks. How do you like working at the bookstore?"

"Just fine." Maybe it's the soft rain tapping the windows, my longing for Connor, or my general sense of disorientation, but suddenly I'm fighting off tears. "My boss arrives from L.A. tomorrow."

"*Acha.* Make him feel at home, and perhaps you will stay a little longer, after I return?"

The heating system hums as the furnace kicks into gear. "I can't. You know that. My clients probably think I died."

"But what about the doctor?"

My heart is suddenly heavy. "I hope I see him again before I leave, but I'm afraid I scared him off."

"Ah, I see." She sounds disappointed, but not surprised. "Look, Bippy, there is something I must tell you, about Ganesh."

"The statue in the front hall?"

"He is all knowing, remover of obstacles. He wrote the Mahabharata with his own broken tusk, but most people have forgotten. He helped me when I was very young, and so I agreed to help him keep the spirit of books alive."

"How did he help you?"

She covers the phone, speaks to someone in a muffled voice, then comes back on the line. "I must go."

"Wait. So Ganesh was your inspiration for opening a bookstore?"

The line is full of static now. "My talent passes down . . . women . . . family . . . inherited. You . . ."

The line goes dead. What on earth is she saying? Nothing I have to worry about now. I need to prepare to meet my boss.

Chapter 31

My second Friday morning in the bookstore, I'm once again dressed in a blue suit and heels. I haven't worn pumps since I arrived. The straps dig into my feet. As I brush my hair, I silently practice my presentation. Soon I'll return to sunshine, palm trees, and my real job. I try to focus on the Hoffman account. I check through the green bar reports, catch up on e-mail, and study stock prices and trends.

When Tony shows up, he whistles. "Whoa, girl. You look like you're headed back to the city." He's in black today, as if mourning my pending departure.

I smooth down my suit and straighten the collar of my silk blouse. "My boss will be here in fifteen minutes. He wants to discuss my presentation."

"I can't believe you're going back to that job so soon." Tony's face falls like a landslide.

"My aunt will return healthy and ready to clutter up the place again." But my throat is dry, and I want to hug Tony. "She belongs here, not me."

"Yeah, whatever." He turns on his heel and strides away, as if I've offended him.

"Hey, wait!" I say, but he has gone into the library. Fine, let him go. I need to focus on my meeting.

When Scott Taylor arrives, he exudes his usual brash confidence, the personality of a boss. I forgot how tall he was, how commanding, although he's slim, narrow shouldered, and not obviously overbearing.

"Hell of a time getting here." His voice projects through the house. He stamps his rain boots on the carpet in the foyer as he snaps shut his umbrella. Water drips from his thin Armani raincoat. He's underdressed for the weather. The soaked shoulders of his jacket have become nearly transparent, revealing the white dress shirt underneath.

"Let me take your coat. I'm glad you could make it."

"Almost didn't. The ferry was running late." He yanks off his wet jacket and hands it to me. I hang it in the closet.

He stares at the statue of Ganesh. "What's the elephant for?"

"He's the Hindu god of new beginnings, remover of obstacles. You kneel, touch his feet, and pray to him."

Scott laughs. "Can he get rid of all this drizzle?"

"I'm getting used to it. I almost find the rain . . . soothing."

"Soothing, huh?" Scott looks closely at me, as if I'm

hiding behind a screen and he can't quite make out my features. "You do look different."

I touch my hair. "Different how?"

"You look good. This vacation is doing you good."

I smile, although I would not call this a vacation. "Thanks for coming all the way out to our blustery island."

"I had a client meeting in Seattle anyway, so I figured I could make a quick detour out here on the ferry. Took longer than I expected." He pats his briefcase. "Where can we get to work?"

"I cleared a space in the back," I say, leading Scott down the hall to the tea room. Now I remember how to walk in these heels. I'm good at it. I don't wobble. I'm smooth on these designer stilts, even if my feet are squished.

He follows, his shoes echoing across the hardwood floor. "I hope you've been preparing your presentation."

"I'm on it," I lie. "Don't worry." My stomach turns upside down. I can catch up, no problem. How could I have fallen behind?

In the tea room, he opens his briefcase on a large table and extracts a few manila file folders. "Coffee would be great," he says.

"Black, strong, no cream, one spoonful of sugar."

"Hey, you remembered." He smiles.

"Coming right up." I pour him a mug of coffee, bring him the mug and sugar, and sit across from him. "How's everyone at the office?"

"Working hard," he says, pulling a sheaf of papers from his briefcase. He doesn't mention anyone else vying for the Hoffman account.

"Carol?"

"She's working on a big one. Now, let's get to the Hoffman account." He pats the sheaf of papers. "We need to emphasize our accelerating returns, diversification. Keep these notes and go through them."

"Sure thing." The papers smell like ink from a copy machine. In a way, I miss that smell. The odor of challenge.

"Let's go over the talking points." He pulls two copies of a memo from his briefcase and hands one across the table. A familiar exhilaration rushes through me. I'm good at making presentations, at conveying the best that our company has to offer.

"I know these by heart," I say, grinning at him.

"You're good. But let's go over this anyway. . . ."

Someone wanders into the tea room—the blotchy-faced man who sought picture books for himself when I first arrived. My heart skips a beat.

". . . returns for equity," Scott is saying.

"Mmm-hmmm." I try to focus on the memo.

The blotchy-faced man looks around, shoulders hunched. He needs help.

". . . and performance reports," Scott says.

"Yes," I say. "I've got it all down."

Tony pops his head in the door and motions to the blotchy-faced man, who then follows Tony down the hall.

". . . when you give your presentation, focus on the chairman of the board," Scott is saying. "I mean, *chairwoman*. She'll have questions. Be prepared."

"I'm always prepared." I strain to hear what Tony is saying to the blotchy-faced man in the hall. I can't make out the words.

Scott taps his forefinger on the table. "Are you with me? You look distracted."

"I'm listening."

"Good." Scott glances at his watch. "Wish we had more time. I have to catch the ferry back. I'll leave the papers with you." He drops his copy of the memo into his briefcase, then gets up and heads to the foyer for his coat. "Review the files," he says on his way out.

"You know I will," I say.

I'll be prepared. I'll blow them all away with my expertise, and Scott will make me partner. The Hoffman account will be the culmination of years of hard work. I'll rake in loads of money and live happily ever after in my new, private condo on the beach, in luxurious sunshine, Robert and Lauren be damned.

Chapter 32

For the next week, I get up early to practice my presentation. I pace in Auntie's apartment, the floor creaking, and talk to myself, gesticulating, using an imaginary pointer. I read every sheet of paper that Scott left for me, memorize every talking point.

Then I walk the beach. I inhale the wild, salty scent of the sea. I don't bring my oversized handbag or my cell phone.

One evening, my parents and I visit the Mauliks again, but the atmosphere is muted, subdued. Sanchita has not returned. Mohan has hired a nanny to help with the children.

I focus on my work, and on reading. I discover H. P. Lovecraft, marveling at his propensity to use big words like *eidolon* and *eldritch* and *Cyclopean*. Nabokov and Wordsworth. I excel at story time, and when the book group meets, I sit with them in the tea room to discuss literature.

Early Sunday morning, a week before I'm to return to California, I carry the memoir Connor's father wrote back into the parlor and shelve it. "I guess he doesn't need another copy," I say to myself.

"I can always use another copy," a deep voice says behind me. I whip around, and there he is, striding down the hall, bringing the smell of fresh air and forest.

My heart kicks up to a frantic beat. The blood rushes through my head. "You're here!"

"I'm glad you're happy to see me." He stands in front of me in a black jacket, cargo pants, and T-shirt, the antique watch on his wrist.

"I missed you."

"I missed you, too." He takes me in his arms and spins me around as if I'm weightless. I'm pressed against his firm chest. I don't want him ever to let go.

I catch my breath after he puts me down. "I thought I would never see you again—"

"I wanted to give you some time."

"You could have called."

"You needed your space."

"I've had enough space." My thoughts are racing as fast as my heart.

"Listen," he says, holding my hands, "let's go away from here, just for today. Unless you have other plans."

"Connor, I—"

"Bring the memoir—I would like to borrow it."

"It's yours." I grab my coat and purse from the closet.

"Wait there. I'll be right back." I dash to the office, running on air, and call Tony at home. "I'm gone today. Can you come in and hold down the fort?"

"Did Connor come back?"

I nod and whisper, "He's standing in the front hall."

"Go for it, girl. Just close the store."

I hang up and race for the front door. Connor's hand is on mine. "Wait. The book."

I retrieve the book and hand it to him. He holds the memoir close to his chest, and the edges seem to glow. The front door swings open, and we step outside into the bright morning.

The wooden porch plank squeaks beneath my feet. Clumps of soft green moss cling to the railing. The sky stretches away in solid blue, scoured clean by the nighttime rain. A soft, cool breeze wafts across my skin, redolent of the salty sea and kelp. All around us are the sounds of morning—a car engine revving, a symphony of birdsong, the rush of the surf. Steam rises from rooftops and fences warmed by the morning sun.

Connor steps outside and takes a long, deep breath. He still clutches the book to his chest. "I love the fresh air," he says in that deep, resonant voice. His irises are deep turquoise, almost unreal.

My heart fills with sweet, pure joy.

He puts the book down on the porch, then stares at his hands, turning them over, as if seeing them for the first time in sunlight. He lifts me into his arms and laughs. "I'm here with you, out in the morning!"

"Yes, you are! I'm glad you're so happy."

"You look beautiful in this light," he says, touching my hair.

"And you, too. I mean, you look handsome." I'm trembling, not from cold.

"I want to explore, live these moments with you. We haven't any time to lose." His wavy hair shines—lighter, sunbleached strands mixed in with the dark. He seems taller, too, and broader, more substantial than he did in the bookstore.

"We could take the ferry into the city. Or stay here."

"Whatever you choose. I want to be with you."

"To the beach," I say. "Come on."

He's right behind me as I run down the sidewalk in my sneakers.

He catches up and grabs my hand. The firmness of his fingers, and the heat, send my heart soaring. I can hear his breathing. "I feel the blood in your veins," he says, squeezing my hand. He throws back his head and laughs. "You make me feel alive, Jasmine Mistry."

I'm awash in happiness. Still holding his hand, I lead him down to Fairport Beach, past Sunday morning joggers, walkers, and proprietors opening their shops for the day.

We're on the sand now, racing to the water, away from the buildings of Harborside Road. A few people dot the beach, and a golden retriever leaps in and out of the surf.

We dodge the waves, laughing. I let go of his hand and dance in circles, collapse up on the beach. He flops down beside me, grabs a handful of dry sand, lets the grains slip through his fingers.

"I want to kiss you again," he says.

"Yes, kiss me," I whisper. This time, I give in to him. The kiss lasts a minute, an hour, forever. Time stops, the seagulls hover, and the ocean waits. I sink into Connor's arms, and then we pull back, gazing into each other's eyes.

"I love kissing you," Connor says, his hand on my chin. "I wanted to kiss you the moment I saw you in the bookstore, looking like a drowned city transplant."

I laugh. "What do I look like now?"

"You're always beautiful." He pulls me close and kisses me again, and then we're up, heading for a rugged stretch of rocky beach. He takes my hand and pulls me up onto a flat-topped boulder. The blood pounds in my ears. I've never felt more awake.

"How did you get so good at climbing?" I say. "You're like a mountain goat."

"I grew up climbing these boulders," he says. "How about you?"

"I grew up halfway across the island," I say. "Near the forest. My parents don't live in that house anymore."

"Do you miss your old house?" he asks as we clamber across the rocks.

"My sister and I planted a garden in the front. Our dad put in a sidewalk. She and I embedded colorful stones in the concrete before it hardened. I haven't been back there in years."

"Why not?"

"I don't know. Childhood seems so far away now."

He jumps down to the sand, then up onto another rock. "Let's go to your old home."

"Now? Today?"

"Why not?"

"Someone else lives there."

"So what? We'll just look."

"I don't have a car. It's too far to walk."

"We'll take bicycles. We can rent them in town." He hops down into the sand. A pristine beach stretches ahead. Not a soul in sight.

"Why would you want to see my old house?" I hop down after him.

"I want to know everything about you." He crouches next to a tide pool carved from the rocks. "Look, there." He points into the water.

For a moment, I see nothing, then an underwater world gradually comes into focus. Orange starfish cling to the rocks beneath the surface. Red starfish. Yellow starfish.

"Beautiful!" I say.

He points at scuttling brown crabs. "Hermit crabs. I'd forgotten how much life is out here." He touches the water with his finger, sending soft ripples across the surface. "This place, the beach, nature. Brings me back to what's important."

"I know. Me, too." We stay for a while, watching the creatures beneath the water, and then we continue down the beach, where large pink crabs crawl in and out of the surf. Perfect shells have washed up, stranded by the receding tide.

"I want this day to last forever," he says on the way back to town.

"Me, too." My heart is full.

In a few minutes, we're in Classic Cycle at the corner of Harborside Road and Uphill Drive, which leads out into the country, toward my old house.

While we're inside the store, choosing bicycles to rent, Lucia Peleran walks in, arm in arm with Virginia Langemack.

"I thought that was you!" Lucia exclaims. "We stopped by the store, and Tony was there. On a weekend! He said you'd be away all day." She sucks in her breath, then holds out her hand to shake Connor's. "My, oh, my, and who might you be? Jasmine caught herself a live one."

"This is Dr. Hunt. He's only visiting," I say quickly. "We have to go—"

"So soon? But why?" Lucia is grinning at Connor.

He nods a greeting and shakes her hand.

Virginia smiles. "Dr. Hunt. The name sounds familiar."

"My father—"

"Yes." Virginia narrows her gaze. "You look very much like him. I remember him vaguely."

"You're a doctor?" Lucia says, her grin widening. Do I detect a flirtatious flutter of her lashes? She's still holding his hand, as if she slapped Krazy Glue on her fingers. "We need more doctors here. We've got everything you need. Culture, art, theater, organic food, lovely beaches. Such beauty here."

"Yes," Connor says, looking at me. "Such beauty." His

gaze makes my knees weak. He manages to pull his arm out of Lucia's grip without offending her. She's still grinning.

"We have to show you around," she says, sweeping her arms through the air.

Virginia is still staring at Connor. "Your father, yes. I remember reading a book he wrote."

"His memoir," I say.

"I may have it somewhere in my library. Funny how much you look like him."

"People say that all the time," Connor says.

"Much mystery surrounding his death—"

But Connor is already steering me to the bicycles, so we can make our getaway.

Chapter 33

The front wheel of my bicycle squeaks, and the gears are stiff, but the sunshine is glorious, the wind in my hair. "I'm sorry about what Virginia said. It's none of her business how your father died."

He pumps up beside me in the bike lane. "I get that kind of question every time someone recognizes me."

"What did she mean about mystery—?"

"Nothing mysterious about losing your father. He died. What else is there to say?"

"I didn't mean to pry."

"No harm done. Let's enjoy this day."

Fine, so he's prickly. I let him be. We pass meadows, farms, vineyards, dense stands of ancient forest. Memories flood back to me, of riding my old bike along these roads, no hands, laughing, reckless. Taking chances. "Down that lane, you'll find the Grand Woods," I say, pointing to the left. "And in that field, there's a Saturday farmers' market through October. To the right, there's North Beach, and Fort Winston, an old army lookout post, is to the west, now converted to a park."

He nods, smiling.

"This way to my old house." I swing left onto shady Rhodie Lane and ride to the end of the cul-de-sac, where the street gives way to a dense forest of fir, cedar, and madrone. As I approach my old address, the palms of my hands grow clammy. Connor is right beside me.

I stop at the curb in front of the house, hop off the bike, and stand there, staring at what was once my childhood home. Connor pulls up beside me. I hear his breathing, smell his sweat, but he says nothing.

Our formerly blue bungalow has been painted drab brown, the wooden blinds replaced by frilly lace curtains. My emotions shift like tectonic plates. "They cut down the blue spruce in the front yard. And we used to have two giant maple trees in the back. We left much of the garden wild. We used to have trees here." All gone, replaced by stunted bushes and manicured grass, artificially weed free. Tears come to my eyes.

Connor rests a comforting hand on my shoulder. "Not what you expected to see?"

I grip the handlebars, as if the bike might slip away. "The only thing that's the same is the sidewalk." The concrete is still studded with the colorful glass beads and rocks. One blue chunk of glass glints in the sunlight, and a memory comes to me. I must have been barely four years old. I'm running along this sidewalk in my summer dress and sandals, *Green Eggs and Ham* tucked under my arm. Dad is driving me to Auntie's bookstore, and I can't wait to exchange this book for a new one. Every time I step into my aunt's old house, Dr. Seuss speaks to me in rhyme. While I sit on the servants' staircase in darkness, I talk to him, and to the other authors whose spirits settle around me like butterflies, telling me gentle stories.

And then the spirits slowly faded, as I grew up, as I spent fewer days in the bookstore, and I forgot the magic.

"Are you okay?" Connor's touching my cheek. His finger comes away wet.

I hastily wipe the tears. "I just . . . remembered something from my childhood."

"Do you want to talk about it?"

I shake my head.

He takes my hand. "We can go," he says gently.

A woman steps out onto the porch in a plaid polyester housecoat the color of lime ice cream. Below the hem of the housecoat, her doughy legs spill down over nonexistent ankles. She bends with great effort to pick up the newspaper from the porch, then goes back into the house. This is her home now.

I turn to Connor. "Yes, let's go. Away. Let's take the ferry into the city."

Chapter 34

Half an hour later, we're on the boat to Seattle, in a booth by the window. Connor sits across from me, his long legs stretched under the table. We gaze back toward the island, at the dense forest tumbling down the hillsides toward a narrow strip of caramel beach.

"Cormorants," he says in wonder, pointing to graceful black birds sunning themselves on a concrete buoy.

"You act like you've never seen them before."

"Not in a long time." He pats the vinyl seat next to him. "Come and sit here. You're too far away."

I move over to his side and, pressed against him, I'm in heaven. How different this voyage feels from the desolation of that ferry ride back to the island a few weeks ago, when I was lost in a stupor of melancholy. My heart is full of the light, the breeze.

We're silent the rest of the way, but I can feel the strong beat of his heart, the line of muscle from his torso to his thighs, the tension of his arm around me.

As the ferry glides in toward downtown, glass high-rises loom ahead of us, and new condominiums sprout up along the waterfront. Giant cruise ships are parked in the distance against the shoreline.

"The Emerald City," Connor says, as people crowd to the exit doors. In a minute, we're out in the cool air, redolent of exhaust and salty brine. We follow the raised concrete walkway that crosses Alaskan Way onto First Street. I'm light on my feet, full of expectation. Connor peers into shops, restaurants, and boutiques as we stroll up to Second Avenue and turn left. We board the free downtown bus in front of the Seattle Art Museum.

We join an eclectic array of the city's inhabitants—an elderly woman; a heavyset man ripping open packs of baseball cards; a girl bopping to music on her iPod. Connor watches them in wonder, as if he is once again in a foreign country.

"Where are we going?" I whisper, thrilled. I haven't ridden the bus in ages, perhaps since my college days.

"Anywhere," Connor says, grinning. The seats are narrow, and I'm squished against him, aware of his warmth. We pass shops, restaurants, cafés. Then Connor pulls the buzzer and we hop off the bus and run up the hill. We're still in the heart of downtown, among historic brick buildings, old corrugated lampposts. We stop in front of the Emerald City Bookstore, the latest releases propped in the window. I'm drawn inside,

Connor at my heels. Fluorescent bulbs cast anemic light across plain bookshelves crammed with new paperbacks. The floor is industrial-strength laminate. Murmured conversation and the generic smells of paper and perfume mingle in the air. In these ordinary rooms, there is no hint of enchantment, no dust or clutter, no plush armchairs or Hindu gods.

"Can I help you?" a round-faced woman asks.

I smile at her. "Thank you, you already have."

She gives me a funny look as Connor and I leave the store. "I don't want my aunt to lose her bookstore," I tell him.

He takes my hand as we trudge up the steep hill toward Seattle Center. "What brings you to this sudden conclusion?"

"Emerald City Bookstore. It's not enchanted. Auntie's saggy armchairs, Ganesh, the pictures on the walls—all the books in piles—everything marks the store as hers. When you walk inside, you know it's her bookstore and nobody else's. It's enchanted. . . ."

"*Enchanted.* An apt word." Connor smiles at me.

We stop in front of a brick corner building with oblong, darkened windows. A small sign next to the door reads *Serious Pie.* "Look, pizza." His voice fills with childlike amazement.

I study his face, the excitement in his eyes. "Don't tell me you've never had pizza."

"Not in years," he says with longing.

"Where have you been?"

"Traveling, remember?" He leads me into the warm, fragrant restaurant with a red tile floor and tall oak tables.

A young, fresh-faced woman rushes up in a white apron.

"Two for lunch? Right this way." She shows us to a table in a shadowy corner. Connor's hand is on the small of my back. He sits beside me and rests his arm on the back of the booth as we share a look at the menu. I can hardly breathe.

"So many options," he says. "If you're vegetarian, you can have the Yukon Gold potato pizza. Mozzarella and chanterelle mushroom."

"How did you know?"

"I see all, hear all," he says and winks.

My cheeks are hot again. I don't remember mentioning that I'm a vegetarian, but I must have. I order the Yukon Gold. Connor chooses the mozzarella and a glass of dark ale.

"So, tell," he says. "Why does a beautiful, successful woman like you return to a quiet island to run a bookstore? What is your real reason?"

Beautiful? Successful? "You flatter me. I told you, my aunt has a heart condition. She went to India for an operation. She's hush-hush about the whole thing. But she called recently to say she's okay. I was worried about her."

"She's an amazing woman. Is she alone in India, or—?"

"We have family there. She's traveling a lot."

"Do you go to India often?"

"I was born there, but I haven't been back since Rob and I met. . . ." Our courtship whirls back to me. Beautiful sunsets, moments I kept in photo albums, in dreams. "He didn't like to travel to exotic countries. He worried about getting sick."

"Now you can travel all you want. You can follow your dreams."

"What about you? What are your dreams?"

He rubs his finger across his eyebrow. "I'm always hopeful, Jasmine. Waiting for the next adventure."

Our pizza arrives, fragrant and hot. Connor closes his eyes while he eats. "Best pizza I've ever had."

"Mine's pretty good, too," I say, but I'm more interested in watching him discover the flavors.

"You know what I want to do?" he says after lunch, as we step out into light again. "I want to see a movie. First one we find."

"Pacific Place, right there," I say, pointing. "They're playing a film noir double feature. I love film noir!"

Both movies are shot in grainy black-and-white with occasional splashes of color. The first film is forgettable, but in the second film, the main character is a troubled, hard-drinking private investigator with a constantly pained expression and a hidden past. He's mesmerizing, but the plot feels incoherent, and I can see the twists coming a mile off. I could watch a dozen incoherent movies, as long as Connor sits so close to me, his knee touching mine. He reaches out to hold my hand, and through every scene, I'm aware of his scent, his breathing, his presence.

How long has it been since I've slept with a man? Nearly eighteen months. My body aches with need.

"What did you think?" he says on our way out of the theater. The sky has darkened, and the air is cool with the promise of evening.

"The terrorism angle felt dropped in, but I loved the actors."

"I didn't notice those details. I just enjoyed the experience."

He's still holding my hand as we stroll down Virginia Street, weaving our way through a colorful city crowd. An Asian man sits on the sidewalk, playing a mournful-sounding stringed instrument.

"That's an erhu," Connor says.

"It's beautiful." I drop a five-dollar bill into the musician's instrument case. Bills and coins pepper the velvety interior. "Makes me feel transported."

"Why don't we transport ourselves to the land of dessert?" Connor leads me into the Chocolate Box, featuring every kind of chocolate, cupcake, and pie in imagination. I choose the rhubarb pie; Connor chooses pear compote. We sit by the window and watch the people pass.

"Ah, pear, my favorite," Connor says, savoring a mouthful. "It's been so long since I've enjoyed fruit this way."

"You were so excited about the pizza, and now dessert. You act like you haven't eaten in years."

"I haven't," he says. "You brought me here, allowed me to eat, to enjoy life for a while. Thank you, Jasmine."

I focus on people passing on the sidewalk. "I didn't do this for you—"

"You did."

"Come on. How?"

"You need me. The power of your heart, of your imagination, allows me to be here for now."

"What are you talking about?" A strange prickle travels up my spine. "What do you mean, 'for now'? Are you going somewhere?"

"I don't want to," he says softly. "Believe me, I want to stay with you forever."

The heat spreads up through my cheeks. The pie seems to grow too rich, too heavy. "Don't talk about forever. Robert used to talk that way. Let's talk about something else."

"All right. Then let's talk about people. I used to play this game. Look at people and try to imagine their lives." He nods toward a man in a suit, carrying a briefcase. "He's a traveling salesman."

I point to an elderly couple in pastel colors and hats, cameras slung around their shoulders. "Tourists from one of the cruise ships."

A woman in rubber-soled shoes races by. "Busy nurse going home from work," Connor says.

A couple saunters past, the man a puffed-up bodybuilder, the woman a buxom blond in five-inch silver heels. Both appear to have visited the tanning salon for countless hours.

"We know why *they're* together," I whisper.

Connor sips his espresso. "Why?" he says, feigning ignorance.

"You know. Just look at them."

"Nothing wrong with a little sex."

I blush fiercely, my lips tingling at the memory of his kiss. "But how long do you think they'll stay together? How long can sex sustain you?"

"For a very long time," he says in a low voice. He kisses me again. I've had it with this trip to the city.

"Your place or mine?" I whisper against his lips.

Chapter 35

Auntie's house is dark, except for the orange porch lamp lighting our way. Upstairs in the apartment, the door is barely shut before Connor is pulling me into his arms. I press my hands into the rough stubble of his cheek, stand on tiptoe to kiss him. I'm in a soft twilight world, falling into a well of sensation, his hands on my hips, traveling the landscape of my body, easing me in a slow dance toward the bedroom.

My nerve endings awaken after such a long sleep, our clothes peeling away like layers of resistance. In the darkness, Connor takes my hand and presses my fingers to a scar on his chest.

I gasp. "What happened? That must have hurt."

"Long story," he whispers. "I'll tell you later. I wanted you to feel this and not be alarmed."

"I'm not alarmed," I whisper.

"That's good." He pulls me onto the bed and into his

arms. He's gentle at first, then insistent, demanding, generous. He speaks to me in a low, rumbling voice, and I throw caution out into the night. I become my deepest, sensual self—I am color, scent, instinct. Connor responds in kind, and we move in symphony.

"You make me feel alive," he whispers, our limbs intertwined, our sweat mingling. "More than alive."

The night passes in a blur. Between frenzied bouts of lovemaking, we share secrets I have never revealed. Somehow, I'm compelled to share my deepest thoughts.

"This is the first time I've done anything like this," I say, lying in the crook of Connor's shoulder.

"You're a wild woman. You must have been a wild child."

"Not really. The closest I've come to wild is playing doctor with Alvin Gourd, the neighbor kid, when I was seven."

"We can play doctor now, if you want."

"I like this better."

"What did you do with . . . Alvin?" Connor says, stroking my hair.

"We took off our clothes and looked at each other with flashlights."

"If you're feeling nostalgic, I'm up for playing that game. Got a flashlight?"

I pat his chest playfully. "You're silly. I wanted to see where all his parts were. Reminded me of shriveled fruit."

"I'm not shriveled."

"Not a bit. You're more like the Superman of the human body."

"Thanks for the compliment, Wonder Woman."

"I did run around in a cape when I was about five. I thought I could fly."

"I wanted to run at the speed of sound," Connor says. "But I was too slow, and I had no muscle. My nickname was Chicken Legs."

"I can't imagine you slow, with no muscles, or with chicken legs. Impossible."

"I changed when I grew up."

"So did I," I say. "When I was little, I thought I heard the voices of spirits. Deep, dark secret. Nobody knows except Auntie Ruma. And now you know, too."

Connor is quiet, his body suddenly tense. "You talk to ghosts," he says finally.

"I've seen them in the bookstore, too. There, I've said it. You think I'm crazy."

"Not at all. The universe is full of spirits. Why wouldn't you see some of them? You're not crazy."

"Robert would say I was. When I confronted him about Lauren, he said I was crazy at first."

"How did you find out?"

"It wasn't any one moment. I didn't catch them in bed together. Nothing so dramatic. It was an accumulation of details. I suspected him for a long time, but I was in denial. I secretly wanted to stay with him. I'm ashamed of that fact. I wanted life to go back to the way it was."

"Nothing wrong with that."

"But that life was an illusion." I sit up and fluff the pillows.

"I pretended I had no clue, but I knew before there was any real evidence. I started checking the numbers he called on his cell phone. I sniffed his clothes, checked his pockets. I even stopped by the university, sat at the back of his lecture halls. I started following him in my car." That desperate woman was someone else, another version of me.

"He forced you to turn into a detective. Who can blame you? He was an asshole. He didn't deserve you."

"Thanks." The room darkens, as if my sadness is leaching light from the stars. "I felt like an idiot, sneaking around. I've never told anyone I did that. Now I've told you."

"You're not an idiot. Not even close." He touches my face, his tenderness bringing tears to my eyes.

"Thanks for being my cheering section."

"Anytime. I can wait on you, too. Are you hungry? Do you want something from the kitchen?" He's getting up, his gorgeous form moving toward the door, sans clothing.

"A slice of cheesecake, but I don't have any."

He makes a magician's motion with his fingers. "I'll conjure one for you. There, cheesecake. Abracadabra."

I press my hands to my cheeks, feigning surprise. "You did it. Wow! While you're at it, how about conjuring some Indian desserts?"

"Like what?"

"*Mishti doi*, a smooth Bengali yogurt. Or *jelabis*—orange, sweet pretzels dipped in syrup. Those are south Indian, but I love them. Pure sugar."

"I'm already in a diabetic coma."

"Or *roshagollas*—breadlike balls of pastry, also dipped in syrup."

"Is there a river of syrup in Bengal?"

"There are many rivers." I watch his profile in the darkness. He seems to be made of many tiny points of light.

"Let's visit one right now."

I lie back against the pillows. "I wish we could. I feel safe with you. But that's silly, isn't it? You could be just like Robert. You could sleep around on me. Go off with another woman. Tell everyone my secrets. You could say, by the way, Jasmine, I made no commitment to you."

"No commitment? We'll see about that." He comes back to bed and pulls me into his arms again, and I'm riding a sailboat on a smooth lake, clear as glass, dreaming, falling, healing.

Chapter 36

As night peels away its veil of darkness, Connor appears almost surreal lying beside me, an imprint of the perfect man summoned from my imagination. Funny, the way his face remains unchanged. The stubble has not grown on his jaw since yesterday. The scar on his chest is a dark dent, jagged at the edges.

What happened to you? I mouth to him silently.

His lashes flutter open, and he smiles at me. How to explain to him the rush of emotion in my heart? "How are you this morning?" he asks in a deep, sleepy voice.

"I'm great. You make me feel beautiful. When Robert left me, I felt ugly. I thought, if only I were more attractive, he would stay with me."

"You're always beautiful. Don't ever question that." He pulls me into his arms, and I snuggle in close.

"When you say it, I believe it."

"Why shouldn't you?"

I nestle in the crook of his shoulder. "Reading about what your father witnessed, and endured himself, in Africa makes me feel that I can survive anything. People have put up with much worse. When I get back to L.A., I'll be able to face whatever comes."

He strokes my hair. "So you're leaving me."

"I have to make a living. I have loose ends to tie up with Robert."

"Then why don't you come back here?"

The possibility had planted a seed in my mind. "On this remote island? This is my aunt's domain. Tell me you'll come and see me in L.A."

He's silent a moment. "I would love to, but—"

"But what? You have other obligations? You're not married, are you?"

"Of course not."

"No girlfriend? Fiancée?"

"No and no. You're suspicious."

"I can't help it."

"One day you will learn to trust again."

"Maybe; maybe not. But I feel hopeful again."

He nuzzles my neck. "And I feel like a living, breathing man. I love the way you smell. I forgot the smell of a woman, and not just any woman. You have your own smell, Jasmine. I could inhale you all day and night." He shifts position so that he's lying on top of me, his elbows propping himself on either side of my body, and for a while, I forget my worries, forget my fears, forget the future. . . .

"How did that feel?" he asks finally, cradling my head in the crook of his shoulder. We're both breathless.

"Out of this world," I whisper. I've given all of myself, and I have survived. I get up, pull on my robe, and open the blinds. "I wish this could last forever."

"I'm here with you now." I feel him come up to me, stand behind me. He wraps his arms around my shoulders. I lean back against him, close my eyes, turn in his arms. Oh, the feel of him, the warmth. He strokes my hair. I look up at him, his face distorted from this angle.

He kisses me again, a long kiss full of promise, full of good-bye. Then he extracts himself from me and pulls on his cargo pants, T-shirt, and travel jacket, as always. Strange for a doctor to wear the same casual clothes every time I see him.

My heart is heavy, and yet, I am also renewed. He comes back to me and takes my face in his hands. "I hate to leave you. What do you want? Tell me."

"I thought I wanted no strings attached. Now I don't want to be away from you." I take a deep breath. "But I've got things to work out, a life to decipher."

"I know you do. You're on your way." He's dressed and ready to go, right down to the antique watch, which needs winding. The hands are stopped at three o'clock.

"I'll come with you this time." In a minute, I'm dressed and following him down the narrow staircase. His outline seems to shimmer ahead of me, as if a miniature sun is shining in front of him.

As we enter the first-floor hallway, Tony's voice drifts from the tea room. He's singing a haunting melody that reminds me of a sad farewell. He must have come in early to do inventory. The lights are on. And he must have left the front door unlocked, although the store is not yet open, because a man steps out of the parlor into the hall. He's dressed in a black T-shirt and camouflage pants, and he's holding a yellow Labrador retriever on a leash—a patient service dog. The man's head is shaved to rival the best Marine haircut. Sweat glistens on his face. His hands are trembling.

Connor holds up his hand to stop me. "Be careful. Don't get too close to him."

"Why not?" But in a moment, I understand.

The man drops to the floor and curls up in the fetal position. He's gasping for breath.

"Sir?" I say. "Are you all right? Can I help you?"

The man moans, but doesn't reply. Tony sings in the tea room, unaware of what is transpiring only yards away.

"Oh, no," I say. "What's happening? Connor, can you help him?"

"Call 911," Connor says. "I have to go."

I tug at his sleeve. "Right now? You can't go."

The man moans, shaking violently.

"Make the call," Connor says, his voice soft, regretful.

My throat dry, I rush for the hall phone and punch in

911. The dispatcher comes on the line. "What is your emergency?"

"There's a man having some kind of an attack." I give her the address and hang up. When I turn around, Connor is gone.

The dog whines and licks the man's face, then paces back and forth, agitated.

Tony bursts from the tea room. "What's going on here? We're not open yet—oh, no! Should I call 911?"

"I already did," I say, looking around for Connor.

A woman rushes down the hall and elbows her way past Tony. Olivia. "I heard someone yelling. Oh!" She sees the man on the floor and presses her hand to her mouth.

"The paramedics are coming," I say. "My friend was just here. He's a doctor. Did you see him? Tall, dark hair?"

"I didn't see anyone." Olivia kneels to read the tag on the dog's collar. "Your name is Hercules," she says softly, patting his head. "That's a good boy. Everything's all right."

Tony runs his fingers through his sprayed hair. "Should we try CPR? I wish I had taken a class."

"The medics are almost here," I say.

A siren wails, growing closer, and then the paramedics arrive, striding in with their equipment. They're asking questions, taking the man's vital signs, moving him onto a stretcher. Tony is talking to them, following them outside.

"I'll watch Hercules for now," Olivia says to me. "Don't worry."

"Thank you, Olivia," I say as she leads Hercules outside. The door closes; I'm left alone. I check all the rooms, but Connor has vanished. Maybe he didn't want anyone to know he spent the night with me. But why? What if he's hiding a secret?

This should not surprise me, after Robert, but I feel as though I've been picked apart, bone by bone.

Chapter 37

"The guy's going to be all right," Tony says in the evening, just before closing.

"What? Who?" I'm dusting the tables in the parlor with a soft cloth, trying to stay busy.

"The camouflage kid. He has post-traumatic stress. Just got back from a war zone. He's going to need counseling."

I fold the cloth into a neat square. "Does he have any family to help him through this?"

"Fiancée, parents. They went to the hospital."

"That's good, that he has a fiancée." Someone to be there for him in his time of need.

Tony grabs his coat from the closet. "You haven't heard from Dr. Hunt, have you? I can tell by your long face."

"Am I that obvious?" I try to smile.

"Stop working so hard. Come out for dinner with me. Forget about Dr. Hunt for a while. He'll come around."

I unfold the cloth and return to dusting. "Maybe he will, or maybe he's like my ex-husband. Maybe I'm a jerk magnet."

"Give him the benefit of the doubt. I'm sure he has a reason—"

"It had better be good. Look, I'll stay here and close up. I'm tired anyway." *And Connor might come back. He has a lot of explaining to do.*

"Do something good for yourself. Soak in a bubble bath. Don't worry about the good doctor. He probably fell for you and freaked himself out. He'll be back."

I wave the cloth at him. "Go on. Get out of here."

"Take care of yourself."

"You, too."

After Tony leaves, the silence is almost unbearable. I should take him up on his dinner offer. Maybe I can catch him before he reaches the ferry. As I stride down the hall, the floor creaks behind me.

"Leaving so soon?" Connor says.

I whip around, my body already at war with itself—flush with relief and at the same time tight with anger. "I didn't hear you come in! How long have you been here?"

"Long enough to hear what Tony said. He's right. I did fall for you. But I didn't freak myself out."

"Then why did you leave? Why didn't you do anything to help that man? Are you not really a doctor?" I press my hand to my forehead. The hall seems to shrink.

"I am a doctor. But I couldn't help." He looks tall and solid, casting his shadow in the hall.

"You could have taken his vitals, at the very least. Why didn't you?" I feel as though I have just stepped onto a moving ice floe. The cold wind blows over me, and every part of me is numb.

"You know the answer. You read my memoir."

"Your father's memoir—"

"Not my father. I wrote that memoir. You admire my father. He is me. Was me."

I grab the banister, hold on for dear life. "But he's dead."

Connor nods. "I was about to come home from Africa. I didn't make it."

"That scar on your chest." I need to sit down. I need air—

"A poacher shot me in Nigeria. This is a gunshot wound, the shot that killed me."

The shot that killed me.

I close my eyes, hoping this moment isn't true.

Outside, the rain splatters down in giant-sized droplets. "You disappear when you step out the front door," I say, half to myself. "You show up at the worst possible moments. I thought it was coincidence. But you were always here." Images of our lovemaking return to me. The places we did it—the positions. I didn't even do those things with Robert.

"The island was my home. After I died, I wandered for a while. Restless. I found refuge here."

"When did you first . . . show up? Why did you appear to me?"

"The first moment I saw you, when you cursed Robert's family jewels, I knew. I knew I had to talk to you. I knew you could see me. You and your aunt share a special talent."

A special talent. Or perhaps a curse. "Were you watching me all the time?"

"I gave you the privacy you needed. You were always safe with me."

"I thought I was safe with Robert, too."

"I'm not Robert."

"I know you're not. But I thought—I hoped—I don't know what I hoped for."

"If I could stay with you, I would. If I could love you forever, I would."

"But you went with me to Seattle. You ate pizza . . . you even had dessert. How can that be?" I wipe tears from my eyes.

"The force of your will, and bringing my memoir out of the store, allowed me to be with you for a while. But that time has passed, and now—"

"Now you have to go," I whisper. Tears blur my vision. "Your watch stopped . . ." *The moment you died.*

Connor takes me in his arms. "Please don't cry. My task was to help you. My last task here on earth."

I press my cheek against his chest. "I don't want you to go. Please don't leave me."

"I can't remain here. I would be nothing but a wisp of smoke drifting through this bookstore forever."

"But I can hold your memoir, carry it outside, and you can come outside again with me—"

"That could happen only once, for only one day."

"No, please. I love you, Connor, I always have."

"I love you, too," he says slowly, "in every moment of light and darkness, in every wink of the stars. I love you when you sleep, when you first awaken in the morning. I love you all the time."

"Then stay!" I hug him tightly. I'm trembling, breaking. If I don't let go, he can't leave.

"I have no choice," he says gently. "Thank you for letting me feel the sunlight on my face, the island breeze, one last time. Thank you for letting me taste the wonder of the life I lost, of love."

"Connor, no." But I have to let him go. He's been trapped here, in this limbo.

"You don't need me anymore. You're strong, so much stronger than you know. You'll be all right now. Don't turn away from happiness. Take the leap."

"You are my happiness."

"And you are mine." He pulls away and rests his hands on my shoulders, but already their weight is dissipating.

Chapter 38

"I wish I could have seen him," Tony says as we wipe down the shelves and windowsills, surfaces that, mysteriously, always end up dusty again. "I can't believe that hunk of a man was standing right there all along. Is he still here watching us?"

"I told you," I say, "not anymore."

"I just can't believe it. You made love with a ghost."

I nod and smile, remembering the fun Connor and I shared, the intimate moments that I hope he recalls in the Great Beyond.

For the past few days, I've jumped at every creak of the floorboards, whipped around when I've felt a breath on my shoulder, rushed into a room if I've heard a voice. But Connor is gone.

"I didn't know it was possible," Tony goes on. "I mean, was he fully functional?"

"Of course he was."

"So exactly what could he do?"

"I'll leave that up to your imagination. That's all I'm going to tell you, no matter how many times you ask."

Tony rolls his eyes. "You're cruel."

"He could do anything a living person could do." I close my eyes and take a deep breath, hoping for a whiff of Connor, a hint of his return. But his scent lives only in memory. His fragrance is gone forever. The shop smells like books, dust, paper, wood.

"You're positively radiant, girl. And your hair, it's shiny. And look at this place. Your aunt will be proud of you."

The store is bustling with customers. Maybe they like the new lights or the spacious, homey atmosphere. I've rearranged the furniture to open up the rooms. Outside, a late autumn sun is shining. I forgot how much I once loved the mottled sunlight, the sound of rustling alder leaves.

"Jasmine, there you are." Lucia Peleran bustles into the store, dressed for takeoff in a white outfit that reminds me of an astronaut. "I've got a special plan, for my future. Could we try again? It seemed as though you almost had something for me before, a cookbook."

"Do you smell that?" I say, turning in circles. A phantom orchard of fruit trees grows up around me, an instant plethora of leaves, sunlight, a harvest of Valencias, tangerines, Seville oranges.

Lucia is staring at me, her mouth slightly open. "What? Dust? This store has always been dusty."

"Not dust," I say. "Citrus. Smells sweet and fresh."

"I don't smell anything." She sniffs the air, an expression of longing in her eyes.

"Listen to Jasmine," Tony says. "She knows of what she speaks."

I choose *The Way to Cook* by Julia Child. "We just got a copy in," I tell Lucia.

She holds the book close to her chest and dances around in circles. "This is it, this is it. Jasmine, you figured it out!"

"Not me," I say, smiling at Julia Child's invisible spirit.

After Lucia leaves, I make a phone call—one I should have made several days ago. Half an hour later, Professor Avery shows up in the store, his hair a gray wilderness. He touches all the books in the Travel section. "So you say you've found what I need?"

Magic in the Mango Orchards glows, as it was always meant to do, and Rudyard Kipling whispers in my ear. *T.S. Eliot misquoted me. I never said that one must smell a place to know it.*

"I hope you enjoy India," I say, handing the book to the professor.

He flips through, his eyes lighting up. "This is the perfect book. The smell! Don't you catch the odors of India?"

"Yes," I say, and I do.

Professor Avery clutches the book in his wrinkled white fingers, as if every hope were concentrated in those pages. "Thank you, thank you!" He can't pay fast enough; he leaves too much money on the counter as he rushes out of the store. Tony chases after him with change.

I pull out Connor's memoir, which is sandwiched between two new books, and carry it back to the tea room. I'm not sure I want anyone else to own this volume. I can keep a small memento of him. The author photo on the back cover looks faded, distant. But I sense Connor watching me from another world.

There's a woman standing in the tea room—a regal, stunning woman in a blue dress. The same woman I saw in the parlor during my first night in the house, during the storm. I recognize her now.

"The descriptions of you, they're wrong," I say. "At least, the ones I've read. That sketch, the last surviving drawing of you. It doesn't do you justice."

She glides across the room, her outline fading, then coming back into sharp focus. "Whimsical and affected, not at all pretty." Her voice is the same one I heard in the laundry room. Musical, dipped in an English accent.

"But you're not whimsical," I say.

"The words of my aunt Phila. She was exceedingly critical, but then what can one expect? And you. You called me plain—"

"You're very pretty. Prettier than your picture."

"Tall and slight, but not drooping? I've also been described in such a way."

"Not drooping at all. Nor plain. Any man would fall in love with you—"

"Every man but Tom—"

"Tom Lefroy? Did he ever come back to you?"

She shakes her head sadly. "Tom and I—it was not our choice to part ways." She glides to the window, turns her back to me. Her loneliness blows through me.

"I'm sorry. I understand loss. We hold on to nothing. Everything we love. Everything that appears permanent. In the end, it's lost."

She turns to me, her eyes brimming with a century of tears. Her outline becomes a yellowed daguerreotype, Jane Austen long gone—an impression only half remembered. "Lost, then found. We love, and we lose, but we can love again." She steps backward, into shadow, until only her face appears like a moon in a dark sky.

"Jasmine. There you are." Tony pops his head inside. "There's a boy here to see you. He said he read the first Narnia book you gave him, and he needs another one."

"Yes, I know that boy. I'm coming." I turn toward Jane, but she's gone, leaving only a soft breeze wafting in through a half-open window.

Chapter 39

On my last day in the store, I'm packed and ready to go. Auntie will return this afternoon. She'll find her precious bookstore still standing, better than it was before. I try to focus on filling orders, organizing the paperwork in her office, straightening bookshelves.

Just before lunch, Virginia Langemack pops her head in the door. I've avoided customers all morning. I'm afraid I'll cry if I say good-bye to anyone. "I hear you're leaving," she says.

I nod, my heart heavy. "I'll miss you all, I really will."

"You can't leave," Tony says behind her.

"Oh, Tony, please don't make this harder than it has to be. I'm sad to leave. I have to catch the boat first thing tomorrow. I hope you'll stay in touch."

"Your aunt would want you to stay," Virginia says.

"I wish I could." I'll soon return to the rhythm of my normal life, and all this—the books, the spirits, the wind-swept island, and Connor—will seem like a dream.

Virginia hugs me. "What's waiting for you in California?"

"My future."

"You've still got the rest of the day here," a familiar voice says behind me. I turn to find a beautiful vision standing in the hall. Wrapped in a verdant silk sari, she brings hints of tropical forest, waterfalls, lilies in bloom. Golden bangles glint on her wrists; she is wearing numerous gem-studded necklaces. Beneath the wrinkles of her tanned face, she glows with newfound joy. Her hair—lush and long—cascades past her shoulders. An aura of sandalwood and faint floral scents surrounds her, and I'm transported to Bengal, to the trains rattling north past mustard fields and into the foothills of Darjeeling, where fragrant tea bushes cling to terraced gardens.

"Auntie Ruma?" I say softly, catching my breath.

She holds out her hands, her fingers heavy with jewels. "Bippy, how lovely you look. My bookstore has healed you."

"And India has healed your heart." My eyes are wet with tears. How can she look so vibrant after what must have been a difficult surgery? I take her warm hands in mine.

"I'm sorry I had to leave you for so long."

A man strides up behind her. Barely Auntie's height, stalwart and handsome, he smiles the dashing, cultured smile of royalty. A handlebar mustache grows thick beneath an aquiline nose. In a tailored black suit, paisley tie, and golden cuff links, he exudes confidence and the scent of fresh aftershave. He's rolling a large suitcase.

"Subhas Ganguli, at your service." He speaks with a rich, smooth Bengali accent. He thrusts out his free hand and shakes mine firmly. "I've heard so much about Ruma's lovely niece."

"Subhas Ganguli?" I say stupidly, staring at him, then at his suitcase, then back again.

Auntie glows.

Tony has come up, followed by a couple of curious customers. "Ruma, you look positively fabulous," he says. "You don't look ill at all. And who is this?" He grins at Subhas Ganguli.

"Tony, my friend," Auntie says, patting his cheeks, "I was never ill. I had only to fix my ailing heart."

Subhas rests an arm around her shoulders and pulls her close to him. "Your heart is safe with me."

I look from her to Subhas and back again. "That's what you meant about fixing your heart?"

Auntie gazes into his eyes, and invisible love hearts fly between them. "It was quite a feat to secure his visa for America. But we succeeded. The wedding itself was far easier."

"Wedding?" I exclaim. My aunt is full of surprises.

Auntie smiles coyly. "You didn't believe anyone could fall in love with your wrinkled old auntie?"

"That's not what I meant." I smile warmly at Subhas. "I'm happy for you. You both must be tired from the journey. I'll make some tea, and you have to tell me everything."

Just then, Ma and Dad burst in the door. Ma's in beige slacks and a matching sweater. Dad's in jeans and a tweed jacket, his hair neatly combed.

"Ruma!" Ma says, rushing to hug her. She stares at Subhas, who politely moves out of the way. "I received your message. You're married. When? Why didn't you tell us?"

Auntie grins. "We knew each other a long time ago, when we were children. Don't you remember, Mita?"

Ma narrows her gaze at Subhas, then her eyes widen, and a look of recognition dawns across her face. "Subhas Ganguli, from the flat across the courtyard? Little pudgy Subhas Ganguli?"

"Mita!" He hugs Ma. "You haven't changed." Then he shakes Dad's hand.

Ma turns to Auntie Ruma. "Why didn't you say anything? How did all this come about? Jasmine, did you know about this?"

"I had no idea." I'm not lying, strictly speaking, since I misunderstood what Auntie Ruma meant about fixing her heart.

Auntie Ruma pats Subhas's cheek. "We wanted a small, private wedding in Darjeeling. Someday we shall plan the big family affair."

"But how—when—did the two of you find each other again?"

Auntie Ruma winks. "Magic."

Ma raises an eyebrow. "Magic?"

Auntie laughs. "This was not sudden. I loved Subhas

even when we were small, playing silly games in the garden. But his family wasn't good enough—our parents thought he had no prospects, or have you forgotten? I followed their wishes, and, well . . . I left Subhas behind for many years."

Ma smiles warmly at Subhas. "We're happy she found you again."

"We're thrilled for you." I hug Auntie tightly, and her joy seeps into me—images of silk and jewels and her dashing Subhas with wavy hair and a handlebar mustache. I picture her smiling in a red wedding sari, resplendent in gold bangles, arm in arm with her handsome new husband.

Dad steers Subhas toward the front door. "You must come to the house for a drink, and supper. My younger daughter, Gita, is coming as well. She would love to meet you."

Subhas nods. "I would be delighted."

Auntie waves her bejeweled arm at Ma. "You go with them. Bippy and I will join you later. We have important things to discuss."

Chapter 40

"Come, Bippy, help me unpack." Auntie drags her luggage up to the attic apartment. Her sari gently swishes on the servants' staircase. The suitcase wheels bump against each step with muffled thuds.

Puffing, I haul the rest of her baggage up after her. "Why didn't you tell me about Subhas?"

"I needed a secret, for once."

"You're sneaky. And why didn't you tell me about the bookstore spirits?"

"I was not at all sure they would visit you. You had forgotten your childhood, you see—"

"Well, they did. The spirits visited me. But you could have explained—"

"If I'd told you, you would not have come."

She's right, of course. "But you owed me the truth."

"Have you not enjoyed your stay?"

"The days have been . . . interesting." And fun. And wild. And crazy. And heartbreaking.

"You must tell me all." Inside the apartment, she glances around and frowns. "I'd forgotten how tiny my home is."

"I've grown to love this place." I cross the living room and set her luggage down in the bedroom. "I'm going to miss the view."

"And what of your doctor? This Connor fellow?"

My heart falls. I tell her about Connor. I'm still talking as Auntie hoists her suitcase onto the bed and begins to unpack. When I finish spilling my heart, I'm out of breath, tears on my cheeks. "I fell in love with him. Isn't that crazy?"

"Not at all. The heart does what it will." Auntie unpacks saris, *kurtas*, woolen shawls. Sandalwood soap. She unfolds a red silk sari, the gold border shining in the light. "Isn't this beautiful? My old wedding sari, from long ago. For Gita."

"It's so beautiful." Memories seep into my bones. Sweet *cha*, dust, the scents of cardamom and turmeric. . . .

"The spirits suggested I give her the sari. What a good idea."

"Do other relatives see the spirits? In India?"

"Only you and I." Auntie unfolds another sari, this one the grayish blue color of the Northwest's ocean at dusk. "Ganesh granted me the ability to perceive the spirits."

I hold the red sari to my cheek. The silk is so smooth, soft. "So now you're going to tell me the story?"

"Ganesh saved my life. I was once married, before I came to America. Before I met Uncle Sanjoy."

"You've been married twice, before Subhas? Ma never mentioned it—"

"Of course she would not." Auntie hangs the dark sari next to a white one in the closet—night and day. "I lived with my first husband for only two months, but he was awful."

"Did he hurt you?"

Her lips tremble, even after all this time. "You know the Mahabharata?"

"The epic—a thousand pages?"

"*Acha.* The Lord Ganesh dropped the book on my husband's head."

"He what?"

"Right on his head. He fell to the floor. Then Ganesh appeared to me in a halo of unearthly light. His rotund belly quivered; his trunk swished from side to side. When he spoke, his voice whispered like the wind in my ear. He said, *Your husband shall hurt you no more.*"

"Oh, Auntie."

"Happened a long time ago, but I remember as if it were yesterday. I remember leaning against the bookcase in our flat. Outside, a bus was honking. My husband was lying on his back, with his arms and legs splayed, his lips already blue."

"The book killed him?"

"Ganesh said to me, *He died of a heart attack.* This is what the doctors determined, in the end. I picked up the book, heavy it was, and returned it to the shelf. I'd already read nearly the entire volume, as I'd been confined to the flat."

"Your husband wouldn't let you leave?" I'm aghast.

"Books were the only luxury he allowed me. And now, Ganesh said to me, *I wrote ninety thousand verses of the Mahabharata with my own broken tusk. And yet people have forgotten, as they've forgotten so many writers after me.* I told him I would never forget. How could I ever repay him? He'd set me free." Her eyes brim with tears.

"Go on," I say softly.

"And so, Ganesh said to me, *You will fulfill your dream of owning a bookstore, but you will be given the ability to see the spirits of dead authors. Your duty will be to keep them alive through their written words, so their books are never forgotten.* I said I would do this with joy. He said, *I grant you this special gift of literary perception, which will pass down through the strong, brave women in your family. Daughter, niece, or grandchild—only the most deserving.*"

"Auntie, this is a fantastic story." And unbelievable. A Hindu god appeared to her and charged her with keeping the spirits of authors alive? They're drawn to this bookstore because of Ganesh?

Auntie wipes a tear from her cheek. "I told him I did not plan to have a daughter. After what I endured at the hands of my husband, I could not imagine ever marrying again. But Ganesh only chuckled. He said, *You will heal, and perhaps you will find new love. Life is unpredictable.* This is what he told me."

"You did get married again. . . ." I run my fingers along the intricate gold weave on the sari. The edges shimmer.

"*Acha.* Ganesh told me one last thing. *Here is my last gift to aid you on your journey. The strength of your will, and an author's book, can bring a spirit to life for a day and a night. Only once. And you will pass this gift to the next woman in line.* Then he disappeared in a swirl of sparkling mist."

"That's a wild story," I say and let out a crazy laugh. My heart is racing, my hands clammy. The memoir. I carried it outside, and Connor was insistent about spending a day and a night with me. "Have you told others in the family?"

"Nobody speaks of my first marriage. It's as if my husband did not exist. I try not to utter his name. Your uncle Sanjoy was good to me, but now I have rediscovered my true love in Subhas. I should have listened to my heart and married him a long time ago, but alas . . ."

"You loved Uncle Sanjoy, too, didn't you?" I say. "Or was the marriage a lie?"

"Not a lie, but a quiet love, the kind of nurturing, easy love that I needed after my traumatic experience. After Sanjoy died, I remained a widow for a decade. But life goes on, nah? And now, I'm ready for the fierce fire of love with Subhas once again. It is possible, I believe, to have love that is nurturing but also fierce. Everything in its time."

I reach out to hug Auntie. I love her scent of Pond's cold cream, her deceptively fragile shoulders. "Thank you for telling me the story."

"The spirits are beginning to fade for me," she says, not looking at me. "I was hoping you might stay."

"Me?" I step away from her, the room suddenly shrinking. "But you belong here. You always have."

Her eyes begin to water. She looks away. "I understand,

Bippy. The store is not doing as well as it once did. Perhaps Ganesh's legacy has ended. Perhaps I will have to sell."

My throat goes dry. "You can make the bookstore turn a profit. I've tried to help things along."

Auntie is silent a moment. "I will stay for as long as I can, and we will see."

Chapter 41

Back in Los Angeles, I stride into the Taylor Investments conference room, set my briefcase on the table, and pull out my proposal for the Hoffman account. The air smells of cologne and coffee beans. I'm surrounded by four men in pressed suits and a woman with collagen lips. White walls, gray conference table, straight lines, and sharp corners. On one wall is my boss's signature abstract painting—a splash of blue and silver like spilled oil on a wet highway. Sunlight filters in through a full-wall window, but the dark glass tempers the effect. Fluorescent lights lend all the faces a greenish tint.

"Henry, are you still playing golf down at the club?" a balding man asks the man next to him, who looks vigorous and artificially tanned.

"I shot seventy-eight yesterday," Tanned Man says. "Can't wait to get back out on the course."

Bald Man presses his forefinger to the table. "Best score for a four-round tournament—seventy-two holes played—was 254 by Tommy Armour III at the 2003 Texas Open."

"I'll take your word for it," Tanned Man says. The others are sipping coffee, shuffling papers, looking at me expectantly.

Scott Taylor clears his throat. "Gentlemen." He glances at Collagen Woman. "Ladies. I believe we're about to begin. Jasmine?"

I stand and clear my throat. "With the new Green Futures retirement funds option at Taylor, you can invest to help the environment. We seek competitive returns while we put your money to work for cleaner air. . . ." And on I go.

Outside the window, a scantily clad woman jogs by, and the male eyes shift. Bald Man taps his pen on the table. Tanned Man casts a quick, sheepish smile at Collagen Woman. She frowns at him. Her face has been lifted, her skin pulled back to keep her future at bay. She gives me an odd sense of sadness.

". . . Our Balanced Fund seeks to promote responsible corporate behavior. . . ." I go on. I find a rhythm. I'm good at this.

Scott keeps a smile fixed on his face.

Collagen Woman raises her hand.

"Yes?" I say.

"This sounds wonderful." She grimaces, and I realize she's smiling. "How do you make sure the firms aren't importing goods from China?"

"We do our best to monitor the companies in which we invest," I say.

"I must say I'm impressed with your presentation."

"Thank you." I'm beaming, and so is Scott.

"Jasmine is brilliant," he says. "She's put in many hours of overtime."

Warmth spreads through me. Collagen Woman nods with approval.

I finish my presentation, shake hands with everyone, and say my good-byes.

"Good job," Scott says, patting my back. "Now we get back to work and play the waiting game."

In my office, I've added a bookshelf full of a variety of novels and nonfiction, a bowl of fragrant potpourri, and plants. But the effect is diluted, piecemeal. I wish my windows opened. I try to focus on work.

An hour later, Scott shows up at the door, grinning. "We did it. They decided right away. We got the account."

I nearly fall out of my chair. "We got it?"

He strides over to shake my hand. "Welcome to the big time. Excellent presentation. Vacation was good for you. This is unprecedented, a client making a decision so quickly."

"Wow. Thanks." My mind is spinning.

"We need to get you a bigger office."

"Really?" I grin at him, surprised. "Thanks."

"Let's talk about strategy. We'll have a company meeting in half an hour. Good to have you back."

"It's good to be back." I did it. I'm good at my job. Maybe I made partner. I can't wait to call everyone I know. Auntie, Tony . . . I wish I could call Connor.

On his way out, Scott glances at the books on the shelves. "I like to read on the plane. Thrillers. 'Course, with the new account, you may not have much time for reading." He winks at me and walks out.

No time for reading with the new account. For some people, reading means the difference between happiness and grief, hope and despair, life and death.

I listen to the office—the whir of the copy machine outside my door, the soft hum of the air circulation and conditioning systems, the metallic ring of the telephone. Voices pass now and then, discussing clients and accounts. The sounds are comforting, familiar.

I got the account.

I try to peruse performance numbers, percentages, line graphs, and pie charts, but I'm distracted. I get up and stand at the window. A white California gull alights on the concrete bench in the manicured corporate garden, a small Eden beneath the palm trees and bougainvillea bushes.

"I got the account," I tell the gull. He looks at me and then takes off. He has a bit of gray on his wings, like the gulls on Shelter Island. Maybe he's looking for the way north.

I imagine the rushing sound of the surf on the island, the changeable sky. Here, a solid block of blue stretches away without end.

Tears come to my eyes. Stupid, silly, unwanted tears, for no good reason. I'm supposed to be thrilled. Now I'll be able to save for retirement, maybe buy another condo.

I rummage through my giant handbag for a tissue to blow my nose. At the bottom, my fingers touch something fuzzy. I quickly withdraw my hand. No movement in my handbag. I reach in and pull out the rabbit ears from the children's book room. Someone must've slipped them in here. The ears are wrapped around the old thin paperbound volume that Connor gave me. *Tamerlane and Other Poems,* by a Bostonian.

Young heads are giddy, and young hearts are warm . . .

My eyes fill with tears.

At the bottom are the words *Calvin F. S. Thomas . . . Printer. 1827.* Was Connor trying to tell me something?

While I work, the poems drift through my head. *The spirits of the dead, who stood / In life before thee, are again / In death around thee. . . .* The tone strikes me as familiar. I need a professional appraisal of the book.

I check the Yellow Pages for antiquarian book dealers, and on my third call, I reach a husky-voiced man who seems to know old books. "What did you say it's called?" he asks, his voice trembling with excitement.

I read the title aloud to him.

"And where did you say you found it?"

I tell him.

"Can you read what's inside? The first page?"

I open the cover with great care. " 'Preface,' " I read. " 'The greater part of the Poems which compose this little volume, were written in the year 1821–2, when the author had not completed his fourteenth year—' "

"I'm going to call another expert. Can you bring the book to me right away? Be very careful with it."

I hang up and glance at my watch. I'm going to miss the company meeting. I tuck the book into my purse and leave the office, turning off the light on my way out.

Chapter 42

I stride off the ferry on Shelter Island on Thursday afternoon. A brisk November wind pushes me down Harborside Road to the bookstore. I'm light on my feet as familiar landmarks rush past me. I'm bursting to tell Auntie what I've discovered.

At the bookstore, she's already at the door in a red sari and Santa sweater, waiting to embrace me. "Bippy, come in quickly." Her face is tight and drawn.

"What's wrong?"

"Such trouble." She pulls me inside, into the comforting smells of dust, mothballs, potpourri.

"What trouble? What's happening?"

"We've got a problem. Ay, Ganesh."

"What problem?"

Lucia, Virginia, Tony, and Mohan are sitting in the parlor.

A hefty, blond policewoman in a blue uniform paces on the creaky floor. Everyone looks worried.

"We have police in Fairport?" I ask, flabbergasted. "What's happening here?"

"Officer Flannigan," the blond woman says, shaking my hand in a vise grip.

"Jasmine Mistry." I let go and flex my fingers. "Is someone going to fill me in?"

"He just disappeared," Mohan says, balling up a tissue in his fist.

"Who?" I say. "Who disappeared?" Did Sanchita come back and then run away again?

"Vishnu. We looked everywhere. He was just here." Mohan blows his nose. Virginia pats his back. Lucia pours a cup of tea and hands it to him.

"When?" I say. "What happened?"

Officer Flannigan steps into the hall to answer a call.

"We came over for story time this morning," Mohan says.

Auntie sits next to him. "Vishnu isn't happy without you, Bippy. When I began to read aloud, he pouted. Then suddenly, he was gone."

"Have you checked everywhere?" I should have explained to Vishnu, said good-bye to him. He has already lost his mother.

Auntie nods. "We looked in all the rooms. We've had everyone out searching the streets."

Mohan clasps his white-knuckled fingers together. "He's become more and more morose."

"How long has he been gone?" I ask.

"Two hours," Lucia says. "Nobody saw him leave the store. One minute, he was sitting in the children's book room, the next minute, he was gone. He was reading Dr. Seuss."

"Wait," I say. "Dr. Seuss? In the children's book room?"

Lucia nods. *The Cat in the Hat.*"

I was Vishnu's age when I ran down the hall, that very book tucked under my arm. I pressed a special spot on the wall, and a door sprang open beneath the stairs. I climbed into the cubbyhole, sat on a pile of old boxes, and pulled the string to turn on the overhead light. I could read in peace, with a sense of wonder. *The sun did not shine. It was too wet to play. . . .*

Dr. Seuss spoke to me then.

"Come with me." I lead everyone down the hall and stop in front of the cubbyhole under the stairs. The invisible door blends into the woodwork.

"What are we doing here?" Mohan says. "You think Vishnu disappeared in the walls?"

I press the edge of the door, and it swings open. Lucia gasps and steps back. Mohan sucks in a breath, and Auntie laughs. "Ay, Ganesh," she says.

"Vishnu?" I call into the darkness.

At first nothing happens, and then, slowly, Vishnu's face appears, moving into the light of a stark lamp that hangs from the ceiling of the cubbyhole. For a moment, he is me, the way I was as a child.

"I knew I would find you here," I say.

"You came back," he says.

He steps out and tucks a book under his arm. A cobweb is stuck in his hair.

Mohan grabs his hand. "Don't do that again. You had everyone scared."

"Sorry, Dad. I needed a time-out."

"Time-out!" Mohan laughs.

Auntie is shaking her head. "We didn't think to look here. I'd forgotten about this hidden place."

"I didn't forget," I say.

"You go, girl!" Tony says from behind everyone else.

We all file into the foyer, and after everyone has left—except Auntie and Tony and me—I produce *Tamerlane and Other Poems* from my purse. I've encased the slim volume in plastic. "A surprise for you," I tell Auntie.

"The Bostonian book!" Tony says.

"What's this?" Auntie asks.

"Not by a Bostonian," I say. "Edgar Allan Poe."

"Poe!" Auntie exclaims.

"Who?" Tony says.

"This is an extremely rare volume," I say. "Connor gave it to me. Poe wrote these poems early in his career, and nobody took any notice. No copies were known until 1876, when one was found in the British Museum. Only twelve surviving original copies are known to exist, and this is another one."

Auntie gasps. "Only twelve!"

Tony is staring at me. "Girl, Connor gave you that book for a reason."

"I've had the authenticity verified," I say. "At auction, this little old book could sell for over two hundred thousand dollars."

Auntie grabs the back of a chair for support, as if she might faint. "Ay, Ganesh."

"Unbelievable," Tony says, letting out a low whistle.

"And so you see, Auntie, we won't have to sell the bookstore anytime soon."

"No, we won't." She presses a hand to her forehead.

I glance at my cell phone display, and there is Poe's face—wide forehead, mustache, wild hair. He smiles at me.

"Thank you," I whisper to him.

"I have but one hope," he says. "I wish I could write as mysterious as a cat."

Chapter 43

Auntie stands at the threshold of the bookstore she has nurtured and cherished for so many years. Resplendent in a purple printed sari and clashing snowman sweater, she hunches against the wind, waving at the crowd in the garden. Half the town of Fairport has braved the blustery weather to see her off.

Stoic, patient, and impeccably dressed, Subhas waits by the black limousine he rented in Seattle, to transport his bride on the ferry to the airport. *Might as well leave in luxury,* he said. Four giant suitcases weigh down the trunk. Ma and Dad and Gita are already in the backseat, perhaps helping themselves to the wet bar.

I'm staying here, where I need to be. If I leave for too long, the bookstore gets cranky. Auntie has left me many of her antiques; smaller pieces have been shipped to India by sea.

At the bon voyage party in the parlor last night, island residents took turns paying tribute to the woman who helped them, who so often mysteriously handed them healing, life-changing books. Auntie thanked them for supporting her store, for giving her cause to celebrate. She introduced me as her successor and assured everyone that I would carry on the legacy of her bookstore.

"Don't let the name change fool you," she said to the crowd, while we all drank wine and feasted on Lucia's baked cookies and scones. "Jasmine's Bookstore will be everything Auntie's Bookstore was, and more. A new era begins."

Everyone clapped and hooted. Ma and Dad beamed, Ma looking triumphant. I've finally come home, where she wants me. Dad wandered off to browse the engineering textbooks, and Gita rearranged displays and decorated the rooms with plants and flowers she'd brought from Seattle. Dilip is away on another business trip. If it weren't for the massive engagement ring on her finger, I could believe that he, too, is a ghost.

Tony got drunk, made a rambling speech, and broke down in sobs. We all comforted him, and he fell asleep on the couch in the tea room, where he is sleeping now. For once in his life, he stayed overnight in the bookstore.

The spirits are behaving themselves, perhaps worried that I may still decide to sell the store. After all, Auntie has paid her debts, still managing to keep some cash from the sale of *Tamerlane*, and she has left the business to me. I hope I can live up to her fame. The town loves her; the tears flow freely as she bids everyone a final good-bye.

"Ruma," Subhas calls, "we've got to go now. We'll miss the flight."

She turns to me and grabs my hands tightly. "Bippy, you must be sure. Are you sure?" Her eyes search mine, perhaps for a hint of indecision. "You don't have to stay."

"I moved in already, didn't I?" I smile at her, but I can't hide my nervousness. "Okay, I'm scared to death. But I'm here."

"You will never be entirely sure of anything," she says, still squeezing my hands. "But we must act anyway, nah? Subhas is not perfect. He is prone to fits of pouting, and he has acquired many other bad habits over the years. I'm not sure, you see, but I must go with him anyway. He is a good man. He loves me."

"You can always come back," I say. "We're here for you."

"*Acha.* I will write you many letters. Your ma and dad are already planning a long trip to India. I have to put up with them for three months, bah!"

"You'll have fun together. I'll miss you so much." My voice breaks, and I wrap her in a tight hug. Somehow I know she will not come back.

"And I you, Bippy. You're the proper successor for the bookstore. You must keep the spirits alive."

"I'll do my best."

"I nearly forgot." She hands me her bundle of keys. "The bookstore no longer belongs to me. You must make it your own."

Through the haze of my tears, Auntie becomes a mirage as she lifts the hem of her sari and walks daintily down the steps.

Chapter 44

The attic apartment affords me a spectacular view of the ocean, the mainland, and majestic Mount Rainier. In the garden, a winter towhee flits through the fir branches. My new cats, Monet and Mary, sit on the windowsill, tails flicking, their green eyes reflecting the light.

I give the kitties breakfast, then make my own. The rituals—feeding the cats, brushing them, and tending to their needs—lift me out of my lonely space. I open the windows to let the rich air fan through the rooms.

"I'm supposed to be here, waiting to become a sister-in-law, right?" I tell the cats.

They purr.

"Connor has gone to heaven or wherever he was supposed to go. And I hope Robert and Lauren are happy in the condo. Maybe I should have asked for more money, huh?"

The cats keep purring.

"They paid me well. Anyway, this house is better than the condo, right?"

More purring.

"Right." I picture Lauren lounging in the sunroom over-looking the sea; for all I know, she and Robert will live there together happily ever after. He can't say I never gave an inch. I've given him more than a mile. Perhaps this twinge, this touch of jealousy, will always plague me, but it comes less often now, and the pain is fading. Time will heal me; time and distance.

"Let it be, right?" I say to Monet. He purrs and stretches his front paws forward, rump in the air. Mary squints at me and hops onto the desk, where she can sit in state to survey her world. No bookstore is complete without literary cats.

I pull on a soft cotton sweater, new jeans, and a new pair of sneakers and brush my locks in the bathroom mirror. My hair is sleek, luxurious.

"This looking glass belonged to me," Emily Dickinson says.

"So Auntie was right." I smile at Emily's austere reflection. Lately, the spirits visit me when I need them, but they don't intrude. "I hope your afterlife is not so lonely."

"Sometimes I engage in lively conversation with Edgar or Charles," she says. "Jane and Beatrix visit me often."

"And Connor?"

"He's gone. Connor no longer needs to be here."

"Of course." If he were here, I would feel him.

I head downstairs to open the store. Monet and Mary pad down after me. Tony shows up in shades of pale blue and green. He wears those colors well. He picks up Mary and cradles her. She goes limp in his arms.

"I have so much good news, I can hardly contain myself," he tells me.

"Spill!"

"I'm in love again." His face radiates happiness.

"You deserve it. Who is he?"

"Someone I met in my writing group, in Seattle. You have to meet him."

"I would love to. Bring him to the store."

"He's been helping me with my manuscript, and now I have an agent. She wants to represent my romance novel." He puts Mary down and she trots off.

"We have to celebrate!" I grab his hands and we dance in a circle. I can hear the spirits laughing.

They help me when a mother comes in wanting a book about how to deal with a crazy teenage daughter; when a grandma looks for a potty training book; when a coin collector wants the next coin book a year in advance of the publication date. Bram Stoker whispers in my ear when a mother seeks the latest vampire novel for her daughter.

For story time I like to choose Dr. Seuss to read aloud. His spirit smiles as I act out the rhymes. My heart fills with joy as I watch the kids' enraptured faces. But I am divided inside, part of me always watching for . . . what?

One Wednesday evening, Ma shows up for the book

group. She joined a few weeks ago; she provides lively counterpoint to Virginia Langemack and Lucia Peleran.

"Sanchita called, but she hasn't come back," Ma says sadly. She shrugs off her coat and hangs it in the closet, then pulls the current book group selection from her purse: *Gone with the Wind*.

"I'm sorry to hear that," I say.

"Mohan has filed for divorce. He's already dating someone new. Can you imagine?"

Somehow, I'm not surprised. "He keeps bringing Vishnu to story time. That's all that matters."

Ma is already striding back toward the tea room. "Are you seeing anyone? Dating?"

"Not at the moment."

"A very nice man will be at the Mauliks' Saturday night—"

"Ma, stop." My voice is gentle but firm.

She shakes her head slightly, but she doesn't press.

Virginia Langemack arrives and engages in a heated debate with Ma about what flowers would work best along the downtown corridor.

Lucia Peleran waltzes in, something different about her, something radiant. "This is my last day at the book group," she announces. "I've got news."

"It's a newsy kind of day," I say.

Ma and Virginia stare at Lucia.

Lucia pantomimes a store sign. "Lucia's Luscious Levain. Come in for your magical muffins and charmed cakes. I'm opening my very own restaurant and bakery!"

Everyone claps.

"Good for you," I say.

"I couldn't have done it without Julia Child. Her book is amazing. Thank you."

"My pleasure," I say.

Julia's hearty laugh reverberates through the rooms.

The next afternoon, I receive my first letter from Auntie on her fragrant pink stationery:

Dearest Jasmine,

Subhas and I are staying in his lovely cottage in Santiniketan (see enclosed snaps). Every morning, we walk to the university and through the nature reserve. We've taken the train into Calcutta— sorry, Kolkata now—to shop at the bazaars. So many relatives have been passing through to visit and congratulate us, I haven't had time to write to you until now.

I miss the bookstore, the customers, Tony, and your ma and dad and you. But I'm happy here, thanks to Lord Ganesh. If Dickens hadn't come to life to walk the earth for one day, and if he hadn't tripped Subhas, then Subhas never would have fallen in front of the newspaper stand. My bookstore was featured in the Times that day.

I neglected to mention this detail. Subhas was visiting Seattle, and when he saw the article on the front page, he knew I was only a few miles away, on Shelter Island.

Thank you, Charles Dickens.

Much love,
Auntie Ruma

So Connor was not the first spirit to step outside, and perhaps he will not be the last.

A few days after Auntie's letter arrives, I receive another, this one from Professor Avery. He now volunteers at an orphanage on the outskirts of Chennai. He fell in love with the director and married her. Together they plan to adopt orphaned girls and establish a network of orphanages. He keeps *Magic in the Mango Orchards* on his shelf—the book that drew him to India and changed his life.

He took a bold leap. And I have, too. I hold on to the sweet memory of Connor. I treasure the gift that he gave me—the ability to let down my guard, to let the castle walls crumble around my heart.

Chapter 45

At the height of a warm spring afternoon, I'm standing in Island Church, a magnificent historic building replete with colorful stained-glass windows. The dais is decorated with a variety of Northwest flowers in bloom.

Dilip's mother has arrived in an expensive mauve silk sari, heavily bejeweled; his father in a tuxedo. They stand with a gaggle of relatives, chatting in animated voices.

Nearly everyone else is here—friends and family, Auntie Ruma and Uncle Subhas, Ma and Dad, the Mauliks, Tony, Virginia, Olivia, and Lucia, who emits the rich scent of chocolate chip cookies. Sanchita is conspicuously absent. She finally sent a postcard from Chennai. She took a temporary job as a pediatrician at an orphanage run by Harold Avery and his new wife. What were the chances? Perhaps she will come to her senses and return to her family soon.

For now, her children, and her parents, must go on without her. They're all here. Uncle Benoy is talking to Dilip. No wonder Gita fell for him. He's solid, squarely handsome, his grin infectious and endearing. He moves smoothly through the crowd, greeting the guests, making them feel at home. He's in traditional clothes, the cream-colored, gold-embroidered *churidar kurta*, the perfect fiancé.

"Jasmine, you look beautiful in that sari!" He takes my hands in his and looks me up and down, smiling.

"Turquoise is my color, I guess." I had trouble wrapping the slippery fabric around my waist—it's been a long time since I dressed in such finery. I'm wearing only a smattering of jewelry. "Lovely day for an outdoor reception."

He lowers his voice. "Where is Gita? She's supposed to be here by now."

"In the dressing room." I nod toward the back rooms. "Ma is with her."

He points at a chubby man dressed in white, standing near the dais. "The priest is here. We need to seat everyone and get started. What's the holdup?"

"Give her a minute. She'll come."

People are taking their seats, murmuring, pointing at the elaborate floral arrangements.

Ma comes running from the back rooms, a vision in a silver sari, except for the tears streaking down her face.

Dilip pales. "What's going on? Where's Gita?"

Ma presses her hands to her cheeks. "Oh, my, she's got cold feet."

I laugh. "Cold feet? Gita? You've got to be kidding. She would have eloped if she'd had the chance."

Ma glares at me. "She doesn't want to come out here. She wants to go home."

Dilip's lips tremble. "I'll talk to her."

Ma lifts a hand to stop him. "She doesn't want to see you."

"But why not? She was all right this morning."

People are glancing over at us. They know something is afoot.

"She's not all right now."

"What did I do? I didn't do anything wrong," Dilip says. "What's gotten into her?"

Auntie glides over in a gold sari and a neon lime sweater. "What's the trouble here?"

We all speak at once. "Gita has cold feet."

"*Acha*, happens sometimes," Auntie says, nodding her head sideways. "Has she vomited?"

Ma gasps. "Of course not!"

"I vomited before my wedding ceremony. Nerves, you know."

Ma wrings her hands. "She was all right when she got dressed. The sari you brought from India, so beautiful on her. And the jewelry. She was smiling—a vision. She loved the henna patterns on her hands. But at the last minute—I don't know what has come over her. Perhaps the wedding is off!"

Dilip sways, as if he might pass out. "Off? The wedding? We've been planning this for months!"

"Ay, Ganesh!" Auntie says. "Perhaps she doesn't want to marry you."

"Get Dad," I say, pointing to the front row.

"She doesn't want Dad!" Ma says. "She wants to leave."

Auntie turns to me. "Jasmine, talk to her."

"Yes," Ma says. "You must convince her to marry Dilip."

"Me?" I'm not the person to convince anyone to get married.

Dilip grips my arm with surprising strength. "Please. I love her." His gaze is intense, pained. "I love her so much."

"Jasmine," Ma says.

My throat goes dry. The priest steps onto the stage.

"She needs her big sister," Auntie Ruma says. "Do what you can."

"Please," Dilip says.

"All right," I say. "I'll talk to her. But I can't make any promises."

Chapter 46

In the dressing room, Gita's collapsed on the couch, curled up in the fetal position. Mottled sunlight filters in through the stained-glass window, making a pattern of watery colors on the hardwood floor. The room smells of perfume and powder and silk.

"You'll wrinkle that lovely sari," I say.

"I don't care." She sniffs, honks into a balled-up tissue. "I told Ma I can't marry Dilip. What if he sleeps around on me? What if he cheats? What if I get pregnant and he leaves me while I'm pregnant? He wants kids and I just picture myself being left alone with them. Day in and day out—"

"Anything can happen, but you can't think that way. You have to believe you'll live a happy, full life. You need to embrace your future."

She blows her nose into the tattered tissue. "What if we

stop loving each other? We have to live together every day, every night, for the rest of our lives."

"What happened to my confident little sister, the one who believes love will always carry her?"

"What if he's not the right guy?" She rips the tissue to shreds. "What if we get married and then he finds someone else?"

I hand her a fresh tissue. "You can't spend your life always wondering what-if. If you love him, and he loves you, that love will carry you. It has to. Otherwise, what's the point in living?"

She sits up and blinks at me. Her eyeliner is smudged, her nose red. "I do love him. At least I think I do. I'm not sure."

"Picture your life without him. Picture coming home and he's not there. How do you feel?"

She closes her eyes. "I feel . . . lonely. I want to hug him and tell him about my day. I want him to hold me the way he does. He makes the best pesto. He whistles off-key in the shower."

"Life is better with him than without him?"

"A lot better. He reminds me of what I can do, that I can make the boutique work. I can expand. I have talent. I don't have to be a pediatrician or surgeon to make a good life."

"He brings out the best in you."

"Yes."

"You love him."

"Yes. But—"

"You know yourself better than you think. You know your heart."

"But you thought you knew your heart, too. You thought you loved Robert, and look what happened."

"Sometimes you have to plunge in, take the risk, grab life with both hands, even if only for a day."

She unfolds the tissue and wraps it around her finger. "Since when did you become such an optimist?"

"Since I met a few spirits who helped me along."

"Auntie's spirits?"

"Maybe, and one of my own."

She gets up and smooths down the sari. "Poor Dilip. I've been cruel, doing this to him."

"He understands. He understands because he loves you."

She glances in the mirror then takes a deep breath. "Hurry, help me fix my makeup and my hair. Everyone's waiting for us."

Chapter 47

After the ceremony, everyone gathers under tents in Fairport Park for the reception. A warm wind blows in across the sea. A band plays softly, and people mill about, chatting, drinking, eating, dancing, and congratulating the happy couple. I've never seen Ma so thrilled. While Gita is talking to friends, Dilip sidles over to whisper his thanks. "I don't know how you did it—"

"It wasn't me," I say. "Gita made her own decision. She loves you."

"Thank you anyway." He rushes off to capture his bride for a dance.

I stand on the sidelines, near the snack table, sipping wine. A couple of men ask me to dance, but I decline. I'll just stand here and get pleasantly drunk.

There's a slight disturbance in the air next to me.

"Excuse me." The voice is rough-edged, arresting. Someone reaches past me to put an empty wineglass on the table.

I step aside, and I'm staring up into the deep blue eyes of
a broad-shouldered man in khaki slacks, white dress shirt,
open windbreaker, his dark hair combed back. His face is
rugged, his skin tanned from the outdoors. He exudes powerful masculinity that stops the blood in my veins. He's not
dressed for a wedding, but somehow, it doesn't matter.

"You're Jasmine, right?"

"Right," I say, nearly speechless. "How did you know?"

"I've been watching you. I have to admit, I asked your
lovely sister, Gita, about you. Beauty must run in the family."

A subsonic wave rushes through me. I nearly drop my
wineglass. "You're bold, aren't you, Mr. . . . ?"

"Giles. Steve Giles." He reaches out to shake my hand.
His fingers are warm, firm, and rough. "Your sister made you
sound intriguing."

I pull my hand away, the imprint of his fingers on mine.
"Oh? What did she say?"

"She said you have a special talent for finding the right
books for people. I'm looking for a guide to the less-traveled
hiking trails on the island." He rubs his forefinger across his
eyebrow in a gesture so familiar, my throat constricts.

"I'm sure I have what you're looking for."

"I'm sure you do." He's watching me intently, studying
me. He gives off a wild scent of the outdoors—at once familiar, yet new and different.

"So, uh, how do you know Gita?" I say.

"She hired me to do some work on her boutique. We knocked out a wall to make the place bigger."

"Oh, you did! In Seattle?"

"Now I've got work on the island. I'm a general contractor."

"You're knocking out more walls?"

"I specialize in historical renovation and restoration."

"So you're renovating something here?"

"Fairport Bed and Breakfast. Quite a project. We match historical details, replace the window sashes, that kind of thing."

"Sounds like intricate work."

"Come by sometime. I'll show you." His smile transports me.

"Maybe you could . . . give me some ideas for renovating the bookstore. It's an old Victorian, a historic landmark."

"It's what I love to do." His eyes are clear blue, leading into forever. "When should I come by?" He steps closer, his outdoor scent, of wood and the wilderness, wafting over me.

"Come by? Um . . ."

"How about right now, after the reception?"

"Right now?" I step back. Connor's voice echoes in my head. *Don't turn away from happiness.* "Okay, sure. That would be nice." I'm blushing.

Steve is still watching me closely. "Want to dance?"

The band is playing a slow song, "Stay with Me."

"I haven't danced in a long time. I'm not sure I remember how. I'll probably trip over my feet—"

"Sometimes you have to take a risk, grab life with both hands, even if—"

"—only for a day?" I gaze into his eyes, and every molecule of my being becomes luminescent.

"I was going to say, grab life with both hands, even if you look like a fool."

I laugh. Inside me, a trapped butterfly has just fluttered free. "All right, Mr. Steve Giles. I will dance with you."

"That's more like it." He puts my glass on the table, takes my hands, and leads me onto the floor. He wraps his arms around my waist, and I lean against him. I can feel his muscles, his strong heartbeat. Everyone else falls away, and we move in perfect synchronicity, just the two of us, dancing and swaying, as if we have always been together.

Readers Guide for

Haunting Jasmine

by Anjali Banerjee

discussion questions

1. Discuss the relationship between Jasmine and her aunt Ruma. In what ways does Ruma serve as a guide to Jasmine throughout the novel, despite the fact that she's in India for much of the story?

2. Throughout the novel, there are several instances in which Jasmine attempts to push herself more toward the back end of running Ruma's bookstore. Why do you think she prefers to work behind the scenes? Do you find her gradual comfort in dealing with the customers telling in regards to her healing from her divorce?

3. Discuss each of the authors who speak to Jasmine during her time working in the store. In what ways do they expose deficiencies in different areas of her life that she didn't realize were hurting? Is there a single message they are each attempting to deliver to her?

4. While catching up with Sanchita, Jasmine notices "a touch of emptiness in her eyes, as if a part of her has vacated the premises" (page 82). Why do you think Jasmine was so sensitive to Sanchita's inner struggle with the direction her life was taking, when her own family members were not? In what ways do you find their situations similar?

5. Discuss the book group meeting at the store. In what ways does this group of women serve as a support structure for Jasmine as she begins to carve out a new life for herself? In what ways does Tony also fill this role?

6. What do you believe was Connor's role in the context of the story? Was it solely to help Jasmine overcome her reticence to open her heart again, or do you think he also served a different purpose?

7. Many literary classics, both for adults and young readers, play an intregal role throughout *Haunting Jasmine*. Do you think that any of the novel's main characters are drawn from the heroes and heroines in the books referenced throughout?

8. How much do you believe Jasmine's culture affects her decisions throughout the novel? Consider the dinner scene with Sanchita, where Jasmine learns she's married to a "nice Indian doctor." Is there any truth to the idea that she may have married Rob partly out of rebellion?

9. Discuss Jasmine and Ruma's "special talent." How much of this do you believe comes from within them, and how much of it is drawn from the store? Do you believe that their abilities help them repair their own lives as well as those around them?

10. Throughout the novel, Jasmine works to land a big account for her firm. Despite her eventual success, she decides to quit and return to Shelter Island to run the bookstore for her aunt. Discuss the different reasons why she chose to do this. Do you think the bookstore now represents a place of comfort in her life? What do you believe were Ruma's reasons for leaving the bookstore in Jasmine's care?

11. Discuss the role of the store itself. In what ways does it almost serve as the main character? Do you think Shelter Island would be the same place without it?